CHICAGO BLUZZ

MOHAN K THANGARAJU

I dedicate this book to my lovely, beautiful, adorable, and angelic
(and no number of adjectives will suffice to describe her)
granddaughter **Poorvi** who has brought new meaning to my
life...our life...and is more than my granddaughter but my mother
and Grand Mother put together...

· Mohan K Thangaraju

Contents

Foreword

Content

Preface

Jonnie aka Janakiraman Sahaskaranamam's dream was to migrate to the United States of America to live the American dream after sacrificing his well-set job with a highly reputed Indian company in Chennai. He gets the opportunity to pursue his dream after getting on to the Y2K bandwagon in 1998 and lands in the US of A with a thud.

He embraces the American life completely from American culture to American whiskey to American women to American weekend to American Shopping etc., etc., and lives his American dream.

What is the dream, he is living?

Jonnie loses his virginity during his second month in the USA and finds love not once, but thrice, all American women. Finds his dream job, gets his green card, big SUV etc.,

Does America embrace Jonnie like he did the US of A? Does it give back to him unconditionally like he did?

How does Jonnie manage the cultural differences? Did all the loves bring him peace and tranquillity?

Did his cross cultural, cross religious marriages hold good? Or create friction for him and his Indian family?

Does Jonnie overcome these challenges and live his American dream or fall back to the Indian Life?

Come on, join Jonnie in his quest to live the American dream.

Prologue

Main Characters

Janakiraman Sahaskaranamam - Jonnie

Abbigail Sara Richards – Abby, Jonnie' first wife, White American

Ravi and Chandran – Jonnie's Indian friends working in the USA

Jennifer and Molly – Abby's friends

Keerthana Parthasarathy – Keethu, Jonni' second wife, Indian American

David Lowry – Jonnie's white American friend

Derrick Manfred - Jonni's black American friend

Malcom – Jonnie's bar tender friend

Sandeep – Jonnie's colleague and friend

Charlotte Lidia Johnson – Charlie, Jonnie's third wife, White American

Surya, Suhasini and Surabhi – Jonnie and Charlie's kids

Sahaskaranamam – Jonnie's father

Varalakshmi – Jonnie's mother

Mansi – Jonnie's elder sister

Subramaniam – Jonnie's brother-in-law

Also, by Mohan K Thangaraju
Novels
One Midnight Summer Madness
Fool's Paradise
Chicago Bluzz
Short Story Collections
Baghala Bath
Happy Ending

ONE

Chapter 1 – Landing with a Thud

I was on cloud nine, not for no reason because I was selected by Gemini Info Tech from Chennai to go to the United States of America to work on Y2K project. US of A, ha...ha...the land of rock and coke (Only Coca Cola). It has been my dream to go to the US for the last several years as many of my friends had gone to the US in the previous years.

My close friends, Ravi and Chandran went to the USA in the last two last years, Ravi went to Boston to work as a Data Base Consultant and Chandran went to Detroit to work on Automotive Electronics and some of my college mates landed in Chicago as EDP (Electronic Data Processing) Engineers for some pharma companies.

I was working for a leading electrical switch gear factory in Chennai and it was a good job with good pay. It was a professional and a prestigious company to work for. My parents and Athimber were dead against me resigning from that company, obviously my Akka too as they were planning to find a suitable brahmin girl so that I get married after a great 'Janavasam'. Of course, it was my Akka's idea seconded by my Athimber and rightfully so. The reason being his younger sister Teju and she was as the right match for me and vice versa according to them.

So, I was stuck in Chennai enjoying movies in Mount Road cinemas and occasional drink in Hotel Ranjith on Kodambakkam High Road. Finally, it was an email from Chandran that broke the spell. Not that the email had any magic content. It was from his

Yahoo mail ID, and the signature at the bottom had this magical line, 'Did you Yahoo today?'. That was the clincher as it appeared to me as an all-American slang and way of life. And I decided that I would go to the US of A soon, not by hook or crook.

It took me almost a year to find the job because many companies felt I was over qualified and doubted why I was leaving such a big company. So, I learnt Sybase, a famous Data Base software too based on Ravi's advice in addition to a NIIT diploma over and above my Electrical Engineering Degree. Then Gemini Info Tech happened to me. They had both Data Base Projects and Y2K projects and decided to hire me as a Senior Engineer to supervise several Y2K projects, a two in one job or multiplexing role in the corporate jargon. They agreed to pay me a salary of $ 3000 per month and free air tickets to travel to India after one-year (if I don't travel, I can encash it), initial allowance to buy appropriate dresses etc., etc.,

It was a good deal according to Ravi and Chandran so I grabbed it despite earning the wrath of my whole family including my Athimber and his family too because his younger sister Teju alias Tejaswini. USD 3000 a month was a big deal with $ 1000 thrown in as travel allowance was bigger than my classmate's deal with Etisalat of Saudi Arabia, therefore I went all out to grab it despite high pressure from my always rational manager and not so rational colleagues (I assume they were jealous of me) plus the most important emotional blackmail by Teju.

'Jonnie, you are due for promotion within six months. Did you consider that before resigning?'

'Sir, I considered that plus everything else...'

'You will become Senior Engineer in Grade E, in the pay grade 15000-500-22000, which means your gross salary will be Rs. 35,000 per month and you will be eligible for a car loan also'

'Sir, I do not want any car loan. This was my dream and let me take it'

'Jonnie, with your promotion you will be deputed to our Powai factory for six months and will get exposure to Schneider Electricals of France's technology which means you can go to Paris on a two years assignment. Consider that...'

I considered that and compared the Land of Rock and Coke and the City of Lights and Love (Paris) and concluded that L of R and C was better that C of L'nL.

Then came the next challenge, Teju.

'Jonnie, do you really have to go to the US?'

'Yes, Teju that has been my dream all these years'

'We can be happy here, you and me'

I did not know how she got the notion and the crush on me, and I guess it was all because of the sincere brainwashing by the family.

'Doing what Teju...?'

'Husband and wife and happily having children, I will be a good wife and mother. Can we not?'

'No Teju, my life is US as of now. Let us figure it out when I come back next year'

And the meeting ended on the expected lines, with Teju crying. I was embarrassed but did not fall for it.

Having won both battles, I decided to focus on the next steps. There were so many formalities to be taken care of, most importantly my USA visa interview. Gemini Info Tech gave a lot of documents apart from fixing up my interview and trained me on the questions to expect and how to answer them to the point. I was told repeatedly not to say anything extra or unnecessary things and stick to the facts. Be transparent and confident.

And there I was at the US Consulate on the appointed time for my visa interview, I was not allowed to carry anything other than the documents and my wallet, not even water. I entered the complex at 11 AM for my 12PM appointment and the image that struck me was that of entering the USA itself, the buildings and the vehicle that were parked were all American. It was a mini-America right in Chennai, right on Mount Road. Wow. That was my first taste of America and I would later go on to learn that Americans always love to carry Home (USA) to whichever part of the world they go to.

The first stop was document verification including fees paid receipts. It took about half an hour then we were sent for bio metric test, photo, thumb impression and iris recording. After all these were over, we were told to march into the main building for the all-important interview.

There were several counters one after another in parallel and about fifty people standing in the hall waiting for their number to be displayed so that they could go to the right counter. I saw folks from all over South India, newly wedded couples with their marriage certificate and wedding album, parents, grandmothers, and youngsters like me.

My number was called finally and I went to counter 8 to face a white male officer dressed in an impeccable white shirt. White American.

I wished him, 'Good Morning' sounding confident and well trained.

He asked in typical American accent that I have heard in numerous Hollywood movies on several occasions.

'Papers please'

I gave him Gemini Info Tech Appointment Letter and the job contract from Data Set Inc., and the work permit application.

'What will be your job in the United States Sir?'

'I will be managing Y2K project and Sybase Database'

'Is it Y2K or Database Management?'

'Both'

'Are you an expert in both?'

'Yes'

'Can you manage both?'

'Of course, that's why I was hired'

'Got it Sir. Tell me something, you do join Data Set Inc., and if they offer you a job once you in United States will you take it?'

'No, I will continue to be the employee of Gemini Info Tech and work for Data Set clients'

'If any of Data Set clients offer you a full-time job, will you take it?'

'I don't know; it is too early to speculate. My focus right now is this job with Gemini InfoTech'

I didn't know then that the term 'I don't know' is a very powerful American term which clinched the deal in my favour. When Americans say I don't know, it means either they do not have a clue or they don't care.

The immigration officer was too good, questioning me like a lawyer. Finally, he said...

'Sir, your visa is approved and you will get your visa in a week's time'

'Thank you, Sir', and I started to leave but could not afford but to follow on the conversations on either side of my counter.

'Madam, with $ 2000 a month your husband cannot support you and your two kids. Your visa is rejected'

I could understand that the wife true to the Indian tradition underplayed her husband's salary which doomed their visa chances.

In the counter to my left, I heard the officer ask, 'So you are visiting your nephew, not son?'

And the applicant was a Senior Citizen and a highly qualified Engineer with over 40 years of experience.

'No, he is my younger brother's son'

'Ah, you are not immediate family. How do we know that you would not start working in United States?'

'No, I am only visiting them as a tourist'

'Why are you traveling alone? Why is your wife not accompanying you?'

'She is an asthma patient, so she can't travel'

'Sorry Sir, your reasons are not clear and therefore your visa is rejected'

I could understand now why getting the US visa is so difficult and why everybody is nervous about attending the US VISA interview. While I felt sorry for those two folks, I was elated because my visa was approved and I walked with a spring in my steps and came out of the Interview Hall and looked around the mini-America inside the consulate once again and said, 'America, here I come...'.

I came out and was immediately mobbed by the auto rickshaw drivers.

'Sir, did you get the visa?'

I was wondering why does it matter to them and the next question explained to me why. I was going to the Gemini Info Tech office near Thousand Lights and told him so.

'Sir, just give me 50 rupees'

The distance is not even 2 kilometres and the bus fare was only Rs.1.50.

'I will give you twenty rupees'

'What Sir, you got the visa and will go to America and you can't even give 50 rupees for the ride?'

I turned down all auto rickshaw drivers and walked all the way to Gemini Info Tech office with additional spring in my steps. After all, I am going to the US of A.

I joined Gemini Info Tech on the appointed date and went through 2 weeks of training on what is Y2K, which systems worldwide have this problem which was all of them, what is the corrective action etc., along with 15 more people and one week of extra training on Sybase. Gemini Info Tech already had more than one hundred people in the USA and I was one of the Supervisors to manage some of those people, therefore I was given additional inputs and training.

I went on a shopping spree and bought the best of the clothes, Park Avenue and Arrow (USA Brand) and packed two suitcases full of clothes and other eatables forced on me like thakkali thokku, oorugai, puliyodarai mix etc., etc.,

Two days before my departure, I threw a party for my friends at our favourite bar at Hotel Ranjith. We started with Bag Piper endorsed by Jackie Shroff and then upgraded to VAT 66, the Superstar's favourite.

My entire family came to the airport to send me off. I settled in the Air India flight and felt like a Maharaja throughout the journey. Twenty-four hours after I left Chennai, I was ready to land in the US of A and got up to retrieve my hand luggage.

I slowly walked in the line after other passengers and came out of the front door and stood there on the ladder and took a deep breath and the cold hit me and I crashed on to the ladder floor with a big loud thud.

****

TWO

Chapter 2 – I have arrived

I woke up to find two pair of concerned eyes looking at me and it took me some time to realize that I was at an American Hospital. I had a drip on my right hand, but bandages and otherwise I felt normal.

One pair of the eyes belonged to an Indian middle-aged gentleman who addressed me,

'Son, you fainted on the ladder due to severe cold exposure. So, I brought you up here'

Then he addressed to the second pair of eyes, a white female nurse', 'I told you, the young lad he will be up soon'

'That's right, pretty remarkable'

I could hear the first part clearly and the second part sounded more like a song line finishing. That was my first real taste of American.

'Janakiraman, I am Rakesh Malhotra. I run a business here in the USA, since you fainted, I had to go through your bag and documents to gather your details and admit you in the hospital. Sorry about that'

I did not know how to answer but just mumbled, 'Thank You Sir'.

'Janakiraman, your company did a good job in getting the Medical Insurance for you. But did anybody not tell you about wearing warm clothes in New York in November?'

'What is warm clothes for November in New York?'

'Thermal wear, sweaters and Leather Jackets....'

'Oh, I have all of them in my checked in baggage'

'Typical Indian… sometimes in November in NY, there could be sudden cold waves'

'I didn't know Sir, but thank you so much'

'You are welcome, Son, do you know what was the temperature when you stepped out of the aircraft?'

'No idea Sir'

'It was 4 degrees centigrade, too severe even for NY'

I just shrugged and asked, 'How long do I need to be in the hospital, Sir?'

This time it was the nurse who responded, 'Sir, you need to be on observation for twenty-four hours and you could be discharged tomorrow if everything goes well'

Again, I understood only half of it and just nodded again.

'Janakiraman, I have already informed your hotel and arranged for your luggage to be delivered to your hotel. So, you do not need to worry about it'

I once again mumbled, 'Thank you Sir'

'Bye for now Son, you can return the jacket when you can. Take Care. I will be in Hyatt Times Square not far from your hotel'

I just nodded and drifted back. So much so, what a way to start my American Dream and I even dreamt of it the whole night. I was driving a red Cadillac with a beautiful lady sitting behind me, who was none other than Julia Roberts and dressed as same in the movie, 'Woman in Red', she was so tempting and I was going to kiss her, then the nurse put a tablet in my mouth. The next minute I was back in the plane and landed in Chennai, and Teju was waiting to receive me, 'Ha, Jonnie, you are back. One year has passed just like this', and she clicked her fingers to demonstrate that. Then I woke up and was jittery for thirty seconds and realized that I was still in the hospital in New York. I was mightily relieved that I escaped from Teju.

I was discharged after two hours that day from the hospital and thankfully my policy cover provided for cashless claim, so I all did was just sign the bill and checked into my hotel, Intercontinental on 42nd Street, Manhattan. My luggage was already there, bell boy brought it up to my room and lingered on for a few seconds and I realised that it is for the tips and I hurriedly took out a five-dollar bill and gave it to him and thought that there goes two hundred rupees. My Indian mind automatically calculated the exchange rate even though my brain was telling me not to do so. But it would take me almost a year before I started converting dollar into Indian rupees whenever I spent money.

I was super exited, took a hot shower bath, changed into denim jeans and t shirt like the Americans, put on my new leather jacket and went out.

I stopped at the reception and asked the black lady at the desk.

'Hi, how do I go to Times Square from here?'

'Hi Sir, you mean you want to get to Times Square? It is easy, just go out of the hotel, head east and after three blocks you will hit Times Square. I will mark the route for you in this map here'

I didn't quite understand head east and three blocks. My Indian mind was looking for directions like go to your right, then third left and walk for two hundred metres etc., And how in the hell I will know the directions N-E-W-S off hand. But it did not take long for me to find out. Every street was numbered and the direction was also mentioned in it, like 42nd Street E and 42nd Street W. So, I understood from the map that the street was running from East to West, in the east end from FDR Hill in Murray Hill/Midtown to West side highway in Hell's Kitchen; another thing I noticed was while even numbered streets were running from East to West, the odd numbered streets like 43rd street were running from North to South. And that was my first Eureka moment in the United States. Walk east, turn north, go straight and turn left. With new found energy I walked towards Times Square encountering people from all over the world, people from Europe, Asia, India, South America, more importantly a of lot Mexicans; people of all colour, creed, and religion.

The whole place was a huge wave of humanity and I was carried by the human wave like it used happen in the Island Grounds during the annual exhibition in Chennai. I passed the famous New York Times newspaper building, and I learnt that the Times Square took its name from it. There were so many street performances by several gangs from acrobatics to group dances to live music performances, all were absolutely enjoyable. Manhattan was full of narrow streets with high rise buildings and that made it different from the rest of the city, and the hall mark yellow taxis were the integral part of Manhattan along with various food trucks that were lined up on the streets. Suddenly I felt hungry, went from place to place looking for vegetarian food but could not find anything. All the food trucks were selling Hot Dogs, Chicken wings, Gyros, Shawarma etc., and there were nice bars located every fifty feet draped in the all-American brown décor. I was getting tired, so I went into one of those familiar looking bars from the Hollywood movies and stood there for a few seconds not knowing what to do.

The black bar tender waved to me, 'Hey Buddy' and showed me a stool at the bar counter. I decided that he is going to be my best friend for the next hour or so and sat down there.

'What will you have?'

'What do you have?'

'Here is the Beer menu and if you want any bourbon just point out to the bottle'. I didn't understand what that was plus there were so many bottles with so many different labels and I hardly knew any of them.

I played it safe, 'What beer do you recommend?'

'Try this Black American Beer straight from the Tap'

'Tap?'

'See here, you want a small or big glass?'

'Small or big glass? I don't know the quantity or size?'

'Where are you from Bro?'

'India'

'First time in United States? No wonder. Small is 12 ounces and Big is 16 ounces'

I again could not convert 1 ounce into ml and decided that I should find about it later.

'Give me 16 ounces please'. I added please after noting that everyone was using 'please' so frequently and everyone was very courteous to each other.

The beer was strong and bitter.

'I am a vegetarian. What vegetarian dish is available?'

'You mean vegetarian food, ha. It could be a challenge. Lemme check with the chef'

He came back with a triumphant look on his face after five minutes.

'Chef says he can whip up a Mediterranean salad with no meat'

His name was Malcom and he became my best friend and we started chatting.

'I see a lot of Indians coming to New York these days. You guys are finding jobs in the United States?'

'Yes, we are working on the Y2K project'

'And what the hell is that?'

I felt like the expert and started explaining.

'All computers in the world have a clock and the time will be reset to 00:00:00 at the beginning of the new millennium. When that happens, the computers will start malfunctioning as they can neither differentiate between year 1900/2000 nor recognize the year 2001'

'Oh, my God. Why is that?'

'Because the date is programmed as 00:00:00 with only two digits for the year instead of four digits and all businesses would be affected'

'Really, like what kind of business?'

'For example, you can't print your bills or receive inventories'

'Even here, this bar?'

'Yes, if you are operations are computerised, your operations will be hit and only businesses that are not computerised can run. But more than half businesses in the world are computerised'

'The how do you fix it?'

'We have to reprogram the date as 00:00:0000 and upgrade software and hardware'

'You mean each and every computer in the world?'

'Yes, there are crores of them and it has to be done very diligently for each one of them'

'Crore, what is a crore?'

'One crore is ten million, never mind what I meant was billions of computers'

'Ha, you Indians are smart, you know many things. But you guys are noisy, litter the place and don't follow the rules', he delivered his verdict finally.

I was not in a mood to argue with him and silently nodded at him. I have heard about the 20% tips of the USA and paid $3 tips on a bill of $7 as I was feeling good. Then I went about exploring the route from Intercontinental Hotel to my office which was right behind the twin towers of World Trade Centre. I Learned a bit about the New York subway train system and what is Line 1 and Line 2 and that routes are named by alphabet such as A, B, C and R etc.,

I found out that it took 25 minutes approximately to reach the WTC and when I reached there, the twin towers looked so majestic and I was awestruck. What I did not know then was that the WTC would be destroyed in one of the deadliest terrorist attacks on human kind killing thousands of people in the near future.

My office building was right behind the WTC twin towers, that was actually Data Set Technology Inc., housed on the 23rd floor with whom Gemini Info Tech had a tie up. I wanted to get my first day on office right unlike my first day on US soil, literally on the ladder, finally I convinced myself that I am ready to start work next day and went back to the hotel peacefully.

The next morning, I reached the office at 830AM itself and was before time. The Manager of that office was Christopher Peterson, a giant white American with speech that sounded like a lullaby. I was introduced to the other team Leads, Dave Lowry, Derrick Manfred, white and black Americans respectively and Sandeep an Indian from New Delhi.

'Dave and Derrick, it's your responsibility to bring Jonnie up to speed because Sandeep is traveling extensively this month'

We came out of the conference room, Dave winked at me and everyone.

'Come Jonnie, let's bring you up to speed'

I did not understand anything and looked confused.

Sandeep jumped in and explained, 'That means to train you fast'

My induction started with a visit to the coffee machine.

'Listen, Jonnie this is the life line of our office. You need to learn to operate the machine and get us coffee every one hour so that we all stay awake'

'First you select the cup size you want. Tall, medium, and big. Tall for Sandeep, medium for me and big for Dave'

'Tall is small...?'

'Yes, it is the smallest'

'Why is then called Tall?'

'I don't know, maybe it is standing tall among the rest. Anyways, coming back to coffee machine, here are the buttons, Decaffeinated, American and regular. You place the cups below the respective slot and press the button. Then add sugar and milk as required. Understood?'

I nodded.

Derrick went on, 'And as it to what each of us drink, medium regular for me with one sugar, no milk; big American for Dave, no sugar no milk; and for Sandeep, tall decaf and two sugar and one milk. Now, just don't stand there. Go ahead and get our coffee'

I stood there baffled and grinned like a dolphin, after a minute everyone burst into laughter and we were slapping each other's back. And thus, started my American office induction. We took coffee to our workstation, which was simply four corners of a large square cubicle with an IBM desktop on each of them. Dave and Derrick took me the through the details of which clients, how many people were working on each client, what level of change was required, what hardware to be upgraded, what software are not compatible etc., etc., they also took me the through the list of floppy drives and what each contained.

I was seriously reading some manual, when I felt somebody slapping me on the back.

'It's time Jonnie boy. Let us go', all three of them were smiling at me.

'Go where?'

'To the Bar, where else? We need to raise a toast to you. Let's go grab a drink...'

'What? It's only 5PM...'

'That's the point, 5PM. We close shop exactly at 5PM. We work only from 9 to 5 and then party after that'

They took me to a nice bar nearby, where they seemed to be regulars as the bar tenders and many of the clients seated there wished them. It was a nice crowd, mix of whites, blacks, Asians, men, women all of them enjoying a drink and camaraderie after work before heading home.

We were seated in a table for four by the window overlooking the street across the Financial District and a white waiter took our order.

'JD on the rocks' said Dave.

'Jack and coke, said Derrick.

'Johnny Walker and soda', said Sandeep.

'And you Sir?'

'What is JD on the rocks?

'Jack Daniels bourbon whiskey topped with ice'

'What is Jack and coke?'

'Jack Daniels with coca cola?'

'Oh, I will also have Jack and coke'

We were sitting and sipping the whiskey and chatting away about everything. Initially I found it difficult to understand what Dave and Derrick were saying because of their accent, slowly I started getting a hang of their accent and later it did not matter as I was thoroughly enjoying myself and reflected on my first three days in the US of A.

Day one, I landed at JFK airport only to faint on the ladder and spent time in the United States hospital, day two I explored all of Times Square, met people from many diverse backgrounds, and day three started off my USA dream. White Americans, black and Hispanics calling me 'Sir' gave me an unnatural feeling and I was carrying $100 in my wallet instead of Rs.1000 and felt rich and I kept asking the question to myself, 'Do I belong here? Am I equal to Americans? Is this my new country...?'

And my mind unequivocally screamed, 'Yes...'

America, I have arrived.

****

THREE

Chapter 3 – Chicago Doll

Time was flying, literally. Before I could realize it was already Christmas and the office started to get empty from 20th December onwards and I was told people would return only after 07th January onwards, till then it was 'Happy Holidays'.

I spent the first six weeks understanding my job, working with Americans, lifestyle in USA, difficulty of being a vegetarian etc., etc., and I ignored Dave and Derrick's advice of working 9 to 5 but worked till 8PM many days so that I could 'come up to speed' as I had learnt. At the same time, it did not stop me from enjoying a drink or two in a week with them.

Two things I learnt about Americans was that they don't waste time while at work, there is nothing like a coffee or a smoke break. It suited me because that is the schedule I followed back at my company in India. Second, they are very good listeners and expect you to keep up your word which was the biggest problem with us Indians. Many of my Indian colleagues would end up saying OK to the clients without meaning it and not deliver as per timeline promised. For Americans when you say Ok, it means you would deliver on your commitment. This was a big cultural barrier and posed a serious professional challenge. Even though I understood the problem, I had not found a solution how to solve it for the team and before I could do so Christmas was on us.

The whole of New York was colourfully lit and looked beautiful and it was already snowing. I was covered in three layers of clothing, first my innerwear, then thermal wear, on top of formal dress with tie, sweater, and full-length leather coat; plus, woollen gloves and woollen cap, adding 5 kilos to my total weight and I still felt cold.

Derrick had invited me to celebrate Christmas with his big family in Buffalo, that is in New York State, close to Niagara Falls. So, I packed my bags and went with him; and what a Christmas holiday it turned out to be. I never imagined that I would feel at home amongst fifty plus black Americans and celebrate Christmas and life, coming from a typical Tamil Hindu brahmin family. Black folks look big and tough but are good at heart, very helpful, close-knit, God-fearing community and are very religious in everything they do including Sunday prayers, community service, caring for the neighbours etc., etc., There are always some black sheep in all communities like all over the world that leads to the entire community being seen with biased eyes.

I attended evening prayers in Derrick's house the first day, and the subsequent days in Derrick's uncle's and aunt's places and every day it was festival like we celebrate Navaratri and Deepavali in India. There were always about fifty plus folks, all close relatives of Derrick in attendance every day, after the prayer everyone raised a toast of wine to the Lord and then started feasting on everything from Beef, Duck, Pork etc., I also joined the toasting and prayed to Lord Shiva, Vishnu, and Brahma silently, after all God's are same and 'Aham Brahmasmi' is the universal belief. Prayer and supper would conclude by 7PM then after an hour's break the drinking would start and go on till 10PM; bottles and bottles of bourbon whiskey would be opened and demolished.

Derrick had about twenty odd cousins, more women than men and one of the women cousins Riley started flirting with me. I was initially uncomfortable, then I got accustomed to it after Derrick winked at me and I started enjoying it. She started sitting next to me during the drinking sessions and used to chat with me nonstop about everything and rub her body on mine in the pretext of reaching for the bottle and sending goose bumps down my belly.

'Jonnie, Derrick tells me you are too good at work. Is it true?'

'I don't know, I just do my work"

'What else are you good at?', the mischievous smile very clearly told me what she was inkling.

'I...I...don't know. Maybe I cook a little bit" and I bit my tongue because of rhyming word that can be used in conjunction.

'Like what?' and she moved very close to me with her busty boobs firmly landed on my upper hand that gave me a hard time, literally.

'Hmm...mainly South Indian dishes like Rice, Sambar, Rasam, vegetables etc.,'

'What is Rasam?', now her hand was resting on my thigh, gently caressing. I almost choked. It was a first of its kind experience for me. I looked at Riley closely, she was attractive in her own way, tall, voluptuous body, big boobs, and thick lips.

'Ha, Rasam is a soup like dish made of lentil leaves, tamarind syrup, pepper etc.,'

I now started swaying to her tunes and my body was moving in her direction and swinging with hers every time she moved. I was breathing coarsely.

'Do you have girl friends?'

"Me, no, no...'

'Really, surprising. No girl friends in India, ok? How about here?'

'Here...no...I have been here only for 6 weeks. No time...'

'Now you have all the time...', with that she put her hand on my crotch making me shudder. She did not stop at that, took my hand, and placed it on her crotch. It felt warm despite the thick denim jeans. I just sat there mesmerised with our drama unfolding below the table.

Suddenly, she declared, 'I am going for a smoke', and stood up. I was relieved. But it was only short lived as she pulled my hand and shook her head that said 'Go'. I got up and follower her. She took me to the sun room at the back of the house and lit a cigarette. Every time she was blowing the smoke, she would open the door and blow outside and close the door immediately. Even that fraction of a second was enough to bring in the cold air to numb my cheek, as result I started massaging my cheeks. Next time, I found my face buried in her big hot bosom taking me to heaven. So, there she was smoking a cigarette and I was breathing in her boobs.

'Oh, poor baby is so cold. Come to Mama…'. She did the boobs burial till she smoked two cigarettes.

Finally, she said, 'Let's go' and took my hand and I was relived only to find it was a short-lived hope and before I could realize she opened the toilet and pushed me inside.

She opened her blouse and loosened her bra to reveal her breasts as big as a coconut, with big dark nipples and pressed my face to them again. By now I started enjoying the physical arousal and kissed her nipples; they were like big black dates. She let out a moan and started rubbing the front of my pant and we kissed passionately, my first kiss in all these twenty-eight years. She pushed me out suddenly and started to unbuckle my trousers and in no time, she had my organ in her hand, rubbed it and moved it back and forth. Then she went down on her knees and put my organ in her mouth and gave me an ecstatically orchestrated blow job. Like in the XXX movies I had watched, she took my semen in her wet mouth to my surprise. Next, she used my hand to tickle her clitoris and masturbated and let out a scream.

That was the day I fully experienced the Free America.

We cleaned ourselves quickly and she announced emphatically, 'Tomorrow, we will fuck' and got out of the toilet only to see Zoe, another ebony cousin of Derrick, standing there. I was shocked and ashamed but she winked at us and went inside the toilet and we went back to join everyone peacefully.

Riley delivered as promised and I lost my virginity the next day, that too in style, in a 1970s Cadillac and on Christmas day with the full blessings of Jesus Christ.

'Hey Jonnie, let's go', this was Riley after supper the next day.

'Wher' thee two of u're goin'?', that was Derrick.

'We are going for a ride till Niagara Falls. I want to show Jonnie, the Niagara in the night without the light show'

'Seriously, in this weather?'

'I am taking uncle Peter's Cadillac, that car heats well', it sounded like a fully loaded statement to me.

Derrick looked at both of us and shook his head as if he didn't believe us.

'Mama, I am taking Jonnie for a ride and be back soon'

'Why don't you take Zoe too?'

'No, Aunty. I am busy here', Zoe nodded to us as if to say have fun.

It was pretty cold in the car, and it took some time for the car to warm up. It was a big, old car but was in decent condition.

Niagara was about twenty miles from Buffalo and it took us almost half an hour to reach there because of the mist.

'Jonnie, you saw Niagara in day time. Now, you will see it in its full splendour with minimal lighting'

'Are we allowed to go there in the night?'

'Yeah, we can, except that there will be no light show like during the season'

She stopped at the entrance road, in front of the half barricade which read, 'No cars are allowed beyond this point, and if any cars pass through, the driver will be ticketed'

Riley hesitated for a second and then put the car in gear and zoomed past the barricade. No sooner than we crossed the barricade, we heard the blaring siren of a police car. She pulled up the car hundred metres from the barricade. The police car stopped 15 feet short of our car.

'Oh my God, it's the cop. Jonnie stay quiet, don't move. Thank God we are not drunk today'

The cop flashed his torch and said, 'Hands where I can see and don't move'

Riley put her hand on the steering wheel. The cop waited for one full minute and then approached the car.

'Mam, do you know why I flashed you?'

'Hmm...I don't know...'

'Did you not see the barricade and sign board?'

'...I...think, I missed it...'

'It clearly says no car can pass through the road after 8PM. But still you went past it'

'Oh, I didn't realize. We only wanted to catch the view'

'There are plenty of other locations here to catch the view. Can I see the papers?'

'Yes, can I get it from the glove compartment?'

'You can, but do it slowly? Is the car registered to you?'

'No, it belongs to my uncle Peter'

'Can I then see your license too?'

She handed over the car documents and her license.

'Sit tight', and he went back to his car.

'He is running the details through his on-board computer to check if everything is in order'

'Hmmm....', the scene unfolded exactly like in the Hollywood movies.

The cop came back after 5 minutes and returned the documents.

'The documents check out and the car is not reported as stolen. So, mam I am not going to giving you a ticket. But you need to be careful next time'

'Thank you, Officer'

He took his car and went back to his patrolling point.

We got out of the car, still shaken and the weather added to it further and we shivered a bit.

'Thank Jesus, I loaded a bottle of Bourbon just in case. Come on Jonnie. Let's take a swig'

We took one sip from the bottle and it helped reduce the tension and warmed us up. After two more sips, we felt better and looked around and the roaring Niagara Falls soothed us further. In the dim light, I could hardly make out the water line but the sound of thousands of gallons of water rushing downstream was unmistakable.

We started walking along the river bed, holding our gloved hands, in spite of the bone chilling cold it felt romantic.

'Riley, does the water not freeze during winter?'

'I dunno Jonnie, but I heard from uncle Peter that it froze partially during some seasons'

'I guess the volume of water is too much and moving fast and then falling over the mountain'

'Maybe...but I have never seen it frozen'

The roaring sound of water rushing and the feeble lights on either side of USA and Canada uplifted our mood and we kissed and she suddenly thrust her tongue into my mouth and sucked my tongue. I later found out that was the French Kiss. We were both aroused fully and rushed back to the car and got into the warm interiors and soon after that I lost my virginity.

We sat inside the car sipping the whiskey and were laughing about the encounter with the cop.

'Hands where I can see...'

I put both my hand on her boobs and she giggled and said, 'Freeze, don't move'. I took it as an invitation to massage them.

'You... naughty man and you need to be punished', and bit my lips. We sat giggling there for some time and made love the second time.

*

The next day I took the flight to Nashville in Tennessee to join my buddies Ravi and Chandran. Riley looked sad to see me go and the entire family of fifty plus folks gave me a warm send off. I felt like Mahatma Gandhi.

'Dude, looks like Riley has taken it to heart. But you don't worry, this is not the first time for her and she will be alright', and he dropped me at the Buffalo Airport.

I boarded the 3-hour flight not knowing what to expect in Nashville. I asked all the questions to Ravi and Chandran on a con-call earlier and they gave me a lot of answers that made no sense to me.

'Machan, what is special in Nashville? Why I can't we celebrate the new year in Times Square?'

'Machi, Nashville is the place to celebrate this New Year, Times Square can wait. Do you know Nashville is the seat of Country

Music in the United States? It's got a great music scene, has so many studios and auditoriums to record songs and for live performance'

'So, are we going to watch live performances only?'

'We will watch a big live performance but don't worry Machi, they have so many bars to wet your thirst and have live music in each of them. We will drink, dance, and freak out'

'What is great about country music? I don't remember listening to any of them'

'Do you remember Dolly Parton? We watched a movie starring her that was a musical in Casino Theatre ten years back'

'Oh, the big tits babe? I remember. Will she also be performing?'

'She is 50 years and old now and we don't know if she is still active but we have booked a show on the 30th that has some big stars performing. Trust us, it will be worth your money'

We were booked in Margaritaville Hotel, a 3-star hotel about 500 meters from Broadway Street which housed all those Honky Tonks bars with live bands. The hotel was very bright and colourful, housing big rooms with two queen size cots; at $60 a night with breakfast for 3 three people, I was told it was a steal.

We did not waste much time in getting into the Broadway Street, which was brightly lit with Christmas lights and looked colourful and cheerful; despite the cold there were plenty of folks on the street, most of them youngsters, walking, talking, laughing, and getting in and out of the bars. When the doors were opened, the blaring music hit us. Everyone was dressed in different type of jackets that made a serious fashion statement.

We got into a crowded bar and ordered our drink. There was a troupe of 5 people performing the so-called country songs, 2 lead singers, one male and one female, one drummer and two guitarists. They were belting nice and peppy songs which uplifted everybody's mood including mine. I couldn't imagine all these years that a 5 people band can perform so well and so fully. I was educated by Ravi and Chandran that country songs used to be sung by farmers at home in the south and central United States and later it was adopted into all the bars to provide entertainment to the peasants while sipping their drinks before going home after a day's hard work in the fields. They all have a couple of drinks, enjoy the camaraderie and the music and then go home for supper.

We started bar hopping and after getting fairly drunk settled in one bar by name 'Acme Seed and Feed' that seemed to be very popular with folks, there were more women than men in the bar. After ordering the drink, I went to the loo as my bladder was too full and about to burst. I noticed while relieving myself, that a lot of toilet tissues were strewn on the floor. Once you are drunk what is America and what is Aminjikkarai, everyone is same. Having realized that philosophy I walked back into the sitting area like enlightened Buddha and fell face down as somebody's leg tripped me.

One pair of rose petaled hands picked me up from the floor and two beautiful green eyes set in an angelic face were looking at me with worry.

'Oh, my God! You are hurt', her voice sounded like music.

And that is how I met my Chicago Doll.

****

FOUR

Chapter 4 – American Tango

'Let me see your forehead, oh...oh...oh... you have a big bump'

She was touching my forehead; her fingers were like ice and my forehead was on fire illustrating the dual nature of life.

My head started to hurt. Ravi and Chandran rushed to the spot.

'What happened Miss?'

'Your friend fell down; fuck...sorry, it was all my fault'

'It's ok, we will take care of him'

'Let me give him first aid, I am a nurse', she took my hand and led me to the Bar Counter.

'Dear, give me some ice, will you... I need to treat this gentleman... and get a stiff whiskey too please'

She applied ice on my forehead very expertly and wiped the dripping water with a tissue.

'I am so sorry; it was so dumb of me to keep swinging my leg, in that manner...'

By this time the whiskey was on the counter.

'Please have a sip, it will reduce the pain. I am Abby, nice meeting you but not under the circumstances, I suppose. And you are?'

'I am Jonnie, these are my friends Ravi and Chandran',

I looked at her more closely now that my pain had reduced and my other senses opened up. She was stunning, typical all-American woman. Sparkling green eyes covered with beautiful mascara, sharp nose with additional slicing of the nostrils that opened up to the sky directly, small, and round lips unlike typical American wide lips that extend up to their ears; normal cheekbones, and blonde hair.

The long fur coat covered most of her figure, whatever was visible looked sexy and I could smell her strong perfume that added to my existing giddiness.

'Hey Ravi and Chandran. Where are you folks from?'

'India'

'I am from Chicago and I see a lot of Indians moving to Chicago these days'

I did not know at that time that I too would be moving to Chicago soon.

'Three more whiskeys please'

We took the whiskeys to their table on Abby's insistence.

'Hey, this is Jonnie, Ravi, and Chandran from India. And this is Jennifer and Molly, my friends from Chicago too'

The ice pack Abby applied really helped and the pain had subsided considerably.

'Where are you folks staying here?'

'Margaritaville'

'Are you kidding...? we too are staying there', they said in a chorus and a big giggle followed all over. All three of them were typical 'I-am-American' type of girls and I could see both Ravi and Chandran too were getting excited. They were quite jealous of my sexploits with Riley and I was happy that now they have a chance of their own.

We partied for some time and went back to the hotel together and agreed to meet for breakfast at 9AM next morning.

We met for breakfast at the appointed time.

'Hey Jonnie'

Abby gave me a hug blowing the wind out of my lungs and then pushed me back a bit to look at my forehead and declared, 'The bump has subsided, that's good. You have balls of steel'.

'What the...?'

'Sorry, I meant you have a strong skull. Come on, let's all grab breakfast'

We all picked up our food and settled down to eat and talked about this and that. I had long back decided that without eating at least egg in the USA, I would die soon of malnutrition and so converted to an Eggetarian.

'Huh, what is the plan for the day guys?'

'Nothing really, just walk around the town a bit and then go to Grand Ole Opry in the evening to catch the concert'

'Wow, we too are going there. What a coincidence?', this was Molly.

'Here is the deal. We are visiting Country Music Hall of Fame after breakfast. Do you guys want to join? Then we can all go together to Grand Ole Opry around 5-ish in the evening'

It was settled and we all trouped down to the Country Music Hall of Fame. Abbi, now owned me and pulled me by hand as she walked and the other four followed us not sure about the pairing between them.

'Gee, I can't believe all of you are Engineers'

'Well, everybody is either studying Engineering or Medicine in India these days'

'Aye, I can understand now. There are several Indian Doctors working in our hospital too and they are very good'

The Country Music Hall of Fame tour turned into a private unpaid special attention guided tour for me, Abbi seemed very knowledgeable about the overall music scene and explained the background and the trophies of various stars exhibited there including Elvis Pressley's gold-plated Cadillac. Our bodies were constantly rubbing each other and the body heat was further enhanced by the indoor heating. I could feel her small but firm breasts whenever we bumped while moving around and turning that prompted me at one point in time to put my hand around her slim Levi's clad hips.

She smiled at me and kissed me lightly on my lips, which were warm and tasted like orange lozenges, giving me a preview of what could unfold in Grand Ole Opry that evening.

Grand Ole Opry was nothing like I imagined, it was a big, completely closed auditorium with a capacity of 5 thousand people and decorated for the festive occasion on the day. Big and beautiful.

We exchanged seats with kind hearted fellow American's and sat together. Abby and I, then Ravi and Molly and Chandran and Jenny in that order; it looked like the jigsaw puzzle between the four of them was finally solved. The Grand Ole Opry diminished in its stature with Abby sitting next to me.

'Ah, you are staying in Brooklyn, awesome place'

'Yeah, I like it too and especially I love the Brooklyn Bridge and the walk back home if the weather permits'

'Seriously, you walk all the way from Manhattan to Brooklyn? You must be mad'

'Not every day, only when the weather permits. Otherwise, I generally take the ferry and then it's a 7-minute walk to home'

"Are you living alone? Or with friends and colleagues?'

'Sharing a flat with 2 more people'

'You good to live with others? I can't. I live alone. Guess I am too independent...'

'I am good for now. Maybe after 6 months I may find my own flat somewhere in New Jersey'

She was originally from Missouri state and her family have been in the timber business for generations; she was the first to become a nurse and move to Chicago from their traditional base of St. Louis. She extracted equal amount of personal information about me and was excited about my 'sacred thread' and demanded to see it right there. Abby was my primary attention and the concert became secondary, and I barely noticed 3 different singers who performed before the break.

We all rushed out to the washroom and then followed a big serpentine queue out in the hall, I initially thought that was a food or snack counter, only to find out it was the queue for the booze. We picked up a double JD on the rocks each and went back to our seats. JD, Abby, and country music were a healthy combination and elevated me to the lunar orbit. We took one sip of whiskey, one sip of our lips. After sipping the live performance, we went back to the hotel and partied on one of the local Moonshine whiskeys in their room till the wee hours of the night.

Abby and I were content in hugging and kissing each other. It was a big relief for me that Abby did not undress and rush me to the bed, had she done, it would have been too much of Free America in one week for me. Thankfully, it was controlled Free America.

Molly and Ravi disappeared into to wash room for 10 minutes, and none of us really noticed as we continued with our sip and kiss activity. We partied so hard for 3 days and were all nurturing a bad hang over and barely managed to stay awake to till midnight on New Year's Eve to shout 'Happy New Year', hug each other, wish folks in the hotel lobby and all that.

Next day, every one was going back to their respective cities after the holiday and we were all somewhat sober and sad. I felt an emotional vacuum to leave Abby and was quick to chastise myself, 'No, it's not anything serious, how can it be? That too with all white American blonde. And I am from India. How will it work out? Sounds preposterous and if I tell anyone, people would laugh at me.

Abby is all American personified, born and brought up in the United States as per their custom, forward looking, progressive with her own set of liberation principles. They know when to have fun and when to be serious and more importantly when not to cross the line, they are trained from childhood to do so because in their Free Society, they get ample opportunities and also chances to cross the line. But in India, we do not get to see the line itself and are told not to venture anywhere outside of home and society (I never figured out the society part) and so when we start in a free society we do not know when not to cross the line and therefore make a fool of ourselves.

I was happy that I was dumb enough not to cross the line with Abby. I was booked in the evening flight and therefore the last to leave. Abby, Molly, and Jennifer took the morning flight as they had to join work from the next day. Ravi, Chandran and I came down to see them off. Abbi gave me a tight hug and we had a lingering kiss and it again rekindled my desire for her. Ravi and Molly were quite normal, so were Chandran and Jennifer. May be Ravi and Chandran were more experienced in USA than I was and therefore knew when to stop. After all, that is what the concept of 'One Night Stand' is all about. Just sex. One night. No emotional attachment. Both parties like, repeat the act when the next opportunity presents. If not, move on.

Abby patted my back and said, 'Bye Jonnie dear, take care', and got into the cab. For a stupid moment, I thought she would look back at me and smile but nothing like that happened. It felt like I was dealing with an Indian woman and kicked myself.

I too went with Ravi and Chandran early to the airport as I did not want to stay back in the hotel alone, it is better to kill 3 hours in the airport than loitering in the hotel lobby. I had about 2 hours to board the Delta Airlines flight, so found myself a seat at the back of a bright bar overlooking not only the bar but that section of the airport too. I was in two minds what to drink, Moonshine or any of the innumerable bourbon whiskeys but during the previous three days I had drunk my one-month quota. My cell phone dinged as I was dilly dallying. It was Abby. Americans are big time texters.

'Hey Jonnie, me settled at home. What are you up to?',

I felt very happy and my inner side woke up. 'This is not just one-night stand stuff, more than that', I thought to myself and I replied to her.

'Hey Abby, in the airport. Waiting for the flight'

'What'ya doin' alone?'

'Deciding what to drink...'

'Oh, I thought you were romancing a blonde:)'

'No, I am missing a blonde'

'Who is that?'

'You'

'Big joke, ha, ha, ha...'

'No, really. Was thinking about you only'

'Don't be kidding. You are a big gun. Smart Engineer, even Doctors will fall for you. I am an ordinary nurse'

It struck me then, that is the deal. I have been thinking what did Abby find interesting about me or her friends about Ravi or Chandran. Smart. Engineer. Great job. Some fancy technology. Y2K.

That's not average American but upper American class, even they are not into high tech, only traditional business. Smart. Engineer or Doctor. That's very much Indian.

'Hey, what's going on Jonnie?', my thought was interrupted and I realized that I didn't text her for two minutes.

'I will settle for the Nurse. Nurses are more caring than Doctors...'

'Liar, liar...'

In the meanwhile, I ordered a strong Moonshine whiskey with 50% alcohol content.

'No, seriously'

'Take care, bye for now. I got to start early tomorrow morning. Keep in touch'

The SMS conversation and Moonshine whiskey elated by mood and I did not mind reaching home late in the night and then slept like a baby.

*

The holidays were over, at least for me. I went to office from the next day even though it was only 3rd of January and there were only a very few people at work. But the coffee machine was on. Quintessentially American. Sandeep, Derrick, and Dave were expected only on 7th but that did not deter me from plunging into work. I reviewed all my projects thoroughly and found more than half of them were behind schedule and did a deep dive of the issues and possible root causes, the Indian company experience of TQM came in handy and I created a tracker with details such as client name, project scope, issues identified, probable root causes, solution that did not work, solutions that worked etc., and found out that people skills issues, high lead time of Y2K compliant hardware delivery, errors during installation of Y2K compliant software and resultant downtime were some of the root causes.

I wanted to find out if other projects too had faced similar issues and if so, how did they manage them. I got access to all the details from the main server and studied them all, surprisingly more than half of them were progressing well, so I added two more column of details to my document that were corrective action and preventive action and then created a cheat sheet kind of document and titled it as 'Y2K Execution – Challenges and Solutions' that ran to several pages, and mailed to all asking for feedback.

Christopher called for a meeting once all supervisors were back in office and asked for everyone's comments and feedback. There were a lot of positive responses as well as new ideas/solutions.

Christopher finally summed it up.

'We all agree this is a good piece of work and can keep all projects on track if the ideas are implemented well and Jonnie has done one heck of a job in creating this 'Knowledge Base'. Well done, Jonnie, I am very pleased and so is the Management. I am going to recommend to my manager that you be rewarded $500 for this achievement'

There was a big applause and multiple congratulations coming at me from all directions. And that was my first rise to fame and there would be many more in my illustrious career later but the first one is always special like the first love. When I broke the news to Abby, she was ecstatic. Less than three months on the job, I became the rock star whether I liked it not.

I was working 10 -12 hours a day, sometimes on Saturdays too when there were issues because my team was working from 20 different locations and I started travelling to St. Louis, Boston, Atlanta, Dallas etc., And I did another thing. All project plans were tracked using Microsoft Excel application and they were lying in the respective desktops making it difficult to view them in one place. I created a Data base using my Sybase skills and created one single database that can be accessed by everyone, the Engineers on the project, Supervisors and Managers etc., and we took it to the clients when there was a dependency on them. I had this DB hosted on a new server with sufficient capacity. This got me the second $500 reward and promotion as the Project Manager from a Supervisor and $300 increment too that led to expected celebration that weekend with all colleagues and well-wishers.

Abby and I had been in touch regularly either through texting or voice messages. She was working for UChicago Medical Hospital in the Paediatric department, UChicago was a top ranked hospital in the country and the paediatric department being one of the critical departments, she was working in shifts and sometimes 24 hour shifts too. That meant she was also very busy but we still found time for each other.

Winter and spring were over in a jiffy and summer was on us, early June and New York was ready to warm. I was told that temperature goes up to 100-degree Fahrenheit plus in east coast in August, the typical Chennai weather I was looking forward to it. I was happy to shed all my warm clothes and dress normally in formals that is formal trouser, shirt and a matching tie and felt I had become lean. Abby and I have been tele-dating for five months now, because of work pressure none us could visit each other either in New York or Chicago. But we still felt connected. Ravi and Chandran started teasing me as the American Devadas.

It was my first summer in the USA, and I too was getting excited and started feeling the festival vibes because that is the only time one can go where they want to, do what they want to do and what they want to wear as the weather is good. All those Jockeys, Nike shorts, sleeveless T's, shoes come out of the wardrobe or be replaced by new ones. Manhattan city park and Brooklyn Bridge were full of joggers in the evening apart from those thronging tourists from all over the world and I enjoyed walking on the Brooklyn Bridge and to home whenever I could and it was very refreshing. I always used to stop midway on the Brooklyn Bridge (Manhattan to Brooklyn) to admire the Hudson River, streamers plying on it, Manhattan Skyline, Manhattan Bridge (Brooklyn to Manhattan) and all the beautiful people jogging in all attractive attires, and the cars going to Brooklyn and back to Manhattan.

It was 6PM during June second week, another enjoyable summer evening with bright sunlight and the sun would set only by 9 or 915PM. Sandeep was in Atlanta, Dave and Derrick were winding up.

'Dude, are you not leaving?'

'No guys. There is only six months to go, and my projects are still at 60% completion. I need to do some trouble shooting this evening'

'So, you will come up with your next research paper and win $1000 reward and another increment. Ha, ha, ha...'

They slapped me on my back and went out singing 'Jonnie Einstein'. I continued to work and lost myself in the work and got up to go to the loo, I noticed the time was already 9PM. I wound up the last of the task I was performing and left office and I was hungry and headed to my day one friend Malcom's bar.

'Yo, how are you today?'

'Yo, I am great Malcom', and we gave a high ten to each other as usual.

'So, the usual?'

That meant Jake and Coke and Mediterranean egg salad. I paid my bill and left by 945PM and started walking to Brooklyn. For a second, I thought of taking the cab, but decided against it to save $20. As I was going towards Brooklyn side the crowd started to thin down. There were only a handful of joggers returning home either to Manhattan or Brooklyn and few last strollers like me. I hit New York Transit Museum at 1020 PM on the Brooklyn side and another 10 minutes I would have reached my flat on 03rd Avenue. The roads were almost deserted and I kept crossing one block after another and suddenly two guerrilla hands pulled me into the back alley with so much force, like I was lifted by a fork lift and placed ten feet apart. Panic gripped me.

'Don' move,' and a sharp object was pricking my neck. It was a big, big black guy.

'Keep your fuckin' mouth shut; else I will slice your fuckin' throat'

He pushed me further to the back of the block away from public view, twisting my arms behind my back and it was hurting like hell. I felt a sudden pain on my nape as the sharp knife point penetrated my nape.

He growled, 'Empty your pockets slowly and keep them here'

I took out my wallet, mobile and handkerchief and placed them there one by one. First, he checked my cell phone, it was a low-end Nokia and he tossed it away with disdain. I could hear the cell phone hit the concrete and break. Then he rummaged through my wallet and took out the one hundred dollars plus cash and pocketed and then took out my debit card.

'You get me $1000 or I will stab you...'

Then he pushed me through the back ally till the end of the block. My panic attack came down a bit, as the physical movement helped me to think; giving him $1000 and escaping would not be a problem but I had $3000 + in my checking account. What if he sees the balance on screen and demands all the money. That was my 3 weeks' salary.

He pushed me to the ATM that was just on the outside corner of the next block and kicked me inside. I was still trembling and dropped the card.

'Pic' it up, Dumbo', growled the grizzly bear behind my neck. I inserted the card and entered the 4-digit PIN with shaking hands and hit the wrong buttons leading to a warning of failed attempt.

'Don't fuck me...', he pushed the knife a little more. I could feel the blood oozing down the back of my neck and I started thinking, maximum wrong attempts before the card is blocked is three, I have already made one wrong attempt, so two more wrong attempts left. I gathered myself and told him, 'Sorry, I typed the wrong PIN'

'Don' mess next time, or else I will chop your fingers', and he moved his big saw tooth knife onto my fingers.

With shaking hands, I slowly typed the second wrong PIN. The ATM beeped and the big black guy screamed and hit me with his back hand. I went sprawling and hit the side wall of the ATM. He pulled me up and hissed in my terrified eyes.

'Next time you fuck up, I am going to cut you in to pieces...you, dumb ass...'

He pushed me again to the keypad; my head was throbbing because of the banging and this time I entered the wrong PIN in a hurry. The ATM beeped the warning and gobbled up the debit card. The big black guy got seriously mad and was shouting, 'I will kill you... I will kill you' and kicked me down.

I doubled up on the ATM floor and quickly formed into a foetal position to safeguard myself and the guy continued to kick me all over the body and his boots were so big and so heavy and every blow was like a hammer head hitting me square. I was moaning and wondering when the hell the beatings will stop. He gave me a final kick on my ribs and stormed out. I lay there panting for a long time and got up slowly. My neck was bleeding and the whole body was aching like hell. First, I picked up the kerchief and applied to the wound and cleaned the blood; thankfully it was a superfluous nick and the bleeding stopped in a bit. I came out of the ATM after picking up my wallet and searched for my cell phone but it was broken and not working, I threw it away dejectedly. But I found a twenty-dollar bill lying there that the black grizzly missed to scoop up in the hurry.

I adjusted my dress and removed my tie, rolled it, and put in my trouser pocket and started walking; first few steps were painful and then gradually it became better and I reached my neighbourhood bar.

'Yo, looks like you have been run over by a truck'

'Nope, by a big, bad grizzly'

'Then you need a drink'

'Not one but two. Give me a double JD on the rocks'

I gulped half of it and felt better as my body shuddered involuntarily and I drowned the rest and went home, took bath, took two pain killers, and slept. It was a fitful sleep and I woke up at 8AM and went to the nearest 7 Eleven and got myself a new mobile phone and called Abby.

She was furious.

'Jonnie, where the hell were you. I have been calling and texting you the whole night. Your cell phone was switched off...' she went on for full five minutes before stopping; women are same whether it is America or Aminjikkarai.

'Nothing Abby, too much of work and I was too tired...'

'No, something is wrong. This is not you. What happened Jonnie?', this time she was worried.

'Well, it is just that…hmm…'

'Tell me honey, you don't sound right…"

Then I told her everything about what happened last night.

'Oh my God. Jonnie baby, that was a terrible thing. Do you feel pain or any swelling in the body?'

'No swelling, but the whole body is acting as if I have been run over by a bull dozer'

'Where are you now?'

'In the 7 Eleven nearby'

'Did you eat something?'

'No, nothing this morning'

'Have some breakfast and take a pain killer, I am coming there'

'No Abby, it is not that serious. One day's rest should be good'

'No Mr. Sahaskara… (that's how she would call me when she was tense in the future) stay at home, I will be there in 3 hours'

She was at home in 4 hours in fact, even to achieve that she must have left Chicago immediately after our call and taken the next flight out of O'Hara International to La Guardia or JFK and dashed to my apartment in the infamous NY Yellow Cab.

Abby was carrying only a small duffel bag and dressed casually in her characteristic blue Levi's denim jeans and beautiful pink T shirt and a matching pull over. She had no makeup and that made her look even more beautiful and stunning.

I was filled with so much emotions.

'Jonnie baby, you are a mess…', she hugged me tightly. This time my bruises hurt unlike in Nashville but still gave me so much comfort; we stayed in that trance for a minute and spoke at the same time.

'It's so good to see you in person after so long…'

We laughed and kissed passionately for a minute and broke up breathlessly.

Abby ran her eyes around the flat and after a full minute of survey said, 'Not bad', in a typical woman's way.

'Come on, let me clean and bandage you', she had brought her nursing kit with her even in the hurry to catch the flight. I was touched by her care and concern.

She made me strip down to my brief and lie on my bed and started cleaning me with usual antiseptic liquid and she was concentration personified and gave a running commentary.

'Oh, so much of bruises. You have taken a lot of battering Jonnie; I never thought you as a physically strong person but you withstood the grizzly attack well. Remarkable. No broken bones, only minor scratches on the face and nape. All will heal in a couple of days'

She applied pain balm all over my body, it was tickling and became erotic a little later and she noticed and chuckled.

'Some body is aroused', and teased me for some time by playing her hands in and around my groin. I felt shame like a puppy and turned to the side.

'Ok, ok Jonnie boy. Mama will not tease you anymore', and she bandaged my nape and applied ointment on my face.

We continued to talk till evening without realizing what time it was and then dressed and went out; picked up Chinese food from a nearby mom-and-pop Chinese restaurant and as an afterthought Abby picked up a wine bottle from 7 Eleven.

We drank the wine in silence looking at each other and ate the food with relish and were feeling good. Almost like lovers. Romantic. Suddenly the other physical urge overtook us; we were at each other with the ever-felt urgency, kissed, and undressed at the same time. I was hard as a rock. Abby had a snow-white lithe body, small and firm breasts with perky nipples and round, perfect ass, and a golden triangular bush below the naval.

We made love slowly and steadily, yes it was a divine experience. Very different from my first experience with Riley. We enjoyed it so much and were resting on each other on the bed.

'Jonnie boy, I have a question for you,

'Hmm... what's that?'

'At what age did you lose your virginity?'

I chuckled.

'Don't tell me this is your first time?'

'No...not really...'

'Then when and where?'

'Well...it was only after landing in United States...'

'Wow, who, when, where...I want to know everything. You better tell me...else, I will kill you'

I slowly blurted out my first experience with Riley in Niagara during last Christmas.

'Ha, ha...Christmas, Cadillac, Niagara...wow. You got taste Jonnie boy'

'No, it was not me...it was all Riley'

'Don't you dare expect this from me. You have to make love to me right here, right now'

We made love again, this time very ferociously and it was again fulfilling and I was on cloud nine and blurted out.

'Abby, I love you...'

'Oh, honey...how I wanted to hear this...all this while...I've bn' waiting to hear this...I love you too Jonnie darling...'

We embraced and smooched each other like kittens and were almost sobbing.

'How I love this moment...I love you with my life honey...'

'I too love you Abby darling with my life...'

And we consummated our relationship by making love the third time that night.

****

FIVE

Chapter 5 – The Knot

We decided to tie the knot. And exchange the ring too.

We have been dating for two years now and last Christmas realized that we would like to become life partners. Abby decreed that we were a compatible couple and said in her typical American style that she would like to get married to me.

We had met in Nashville during New Year eve two and a half years back and a lot of water has flown under the bridge since then.

We visited Abby's parents last Christmas in St. Louis after her persistent bidding. I was not sure how I would handle their parents and brothers; had it been India I would have some idea about what to expect, positives, negatives and objections but here I had no clue how to handle the American parents reacting to the inter religion and inter race marriage proposal. Hollywood had unfortunately failed to educate me on this topic. Abby's parents and elder brother were living in Lindbergh on the outskirts of St. Louis; they were into timber business for generations with 100 years lease from Missouri state for planting oak and felling them for timber over 100 hectares and they had their big timber store close to I – 55 not far from their house. Their home was a beautiful French style country house of over 4000 square feet built up area on a 10,000 square feet land, five bedrooms spread over the basement to the first floor, ample living area with spacious kitchen and dining area with the bar right in the dining area, for easy access and greater fun. They had 1000 square feet of Barbeque Stage behind the house like every American household and 2000 square feet of lush grass below that. They owned 2 big Ford F 110 pick-up trucks and a Cadillac SUV, the formers used by Abby's father and elder brother respectively and the Cadillac driven predominantly by Abby and her younger brothers whenever they were home.

Her father was a huge guy weighing close to 300 pounds and towering over 6 feet, in his early fifties with a big moustache or whiskers typical of mid-western America, and her mother too was tall, slender and a handsome woman in her late forties. Abby herself was a tall woman, I have to admit now that she is two inches taller than I, 5'9" to my 5'7". Her father's name is Liam Montgomery Richards Sr., I guess he became senior after naming his first son as Liam Montgomery Richards Jr.,

Abby's parents and her elder brother received me well but her younger brothers gave me a hostile look because Abby was their angel and loving big sister, they adored her; in fact, Abby was the pet and favourite of everyone being the only girl child and of course she was throwing her tantrums always. Now I understood how and where she got her tantrums and attention seeking habit.

Rich, her elder brother, and I got along well, maybe because we were of the same age; her parents did not show any sign of surprise of having their only daughter's Indian boyfriend at home for Christmas despite it being a family affair. I did not know what conversation took place between Abby' parents and her, but whatever apprehensions they had they did not show any sign of that. I could detect a bit of respect for what I was, a highly qualified Engineer working for an American MNC plus I have now become more or less American two years after embracing American lifestyle and lingo, I was kind of rolling my R's and finishing my sentences in a lullaby like Americans do, otherwise they were finding it difficult to understand me otherwise.

I accompanied them to church for the Christmas evening prayer.

Her father was very understanding, 'Jonnie, we would understand it perfectly well in case you do not wish to join us'.

'Sir, I don't have any issues as I believe GOD is one be it Lord Shiva, Jesus Christ or Allah'

'That's very good of you to say. You don't have come inside the church if you don't want to...'

'I don't mind entering the church, maybe I will sit in the last bench to escape the cold while you folks pray'

My humour attempt to lighten the situation went well with the family; her father gave me an appreciating look.

We were all sitting at the big dining table back home from the church and toasted each other and drank wine like as it happened during the Last Supper. While they feasted on roast turkey, pulled chicken and steak accompanied by a mountain of salad and big, fresh home baked bread, I was content with the bread, soup, and the salad. After dinner, we all adjourned to the Sun Room at the back for a smoke and coffee. Abby's father was smoking a cigar and Rick and Abby smoked Marlboro; her younger brothers did not smoke at home respecting the parents and family.

'Jonnie, which city your parents live?'

'They live in Chennai City, in the state of Tamil Nadu in South India'

'Oh, ok...I don't know where it is to be honest'

'No worries, Mr. Richards. And my elder Sister and brother-in-law, too live in the same city'

'And what's the weather like? Is it cold in the winter like here?'

'No, it has one only climate. Hot and Hotter. There is really no winter as it is more or less halfway between the Equator and Tropic of Cancer'

'Oh, I see...hmm...you seem to know the geography really well...'

'It's nothing, we study geography extensively in the school and by the time we finish school it transforms into general knowledge'

Then it was time for the whiskeys, best of the bourbon bottles were brought to the table and we drank our fill, chatted about snow covering the road to timber business, my work, Abby's work, and her younger brothers' studies etc., etc., then we all retired to our respective rooms.

Abby was in her flirtatious and seductive best, therefore not having sex was not a choice even after good drinking. Another

American or western habit. We made love passionately and slowly, our love making sessions have graduated from rip your clothes and fuck to kiss, undress each other, hugging, cuddling, enough foreplay before the climax.

We were resting on each other for a while and Abby poured one shot of Woodford Reserve whiskey and started sipping it while savouring the nose, palette and finish like they always describe the whiskeys.

Suddenly Abby said, 'Honey, I think I am ready'

'Ready for what dear?

'Ready to get married to you!'

I was taken aback, to be honest even I was thinking about it for quiet sometime.

'Abby, are you serious? Or you playing a prank?'

'No honey, I am serious. I guess it is time for us to get married and be an official couple'

'I think you are drunk and blabbering...'

'You dare not call me drunk Mr. Sahas...I am sober as ever and I mean it...'

When she gets high, feels sudden burst of love or gets angry she addresses me like that.

'I get it baby. Let me sleep on in it and we can talk it out in the morning'

'As you say honey...'

The next morning before we went down for breakfast, I declared, 'Abby, I too want to get married to you'

She was ecstatic and kissed me passionately. We went down and joined everybody at the breakfast table and suddenly Abby stood up while breakfast session was on.

'Hello everyone, we have an announcement to make...Daddy, mummy, Ricky, and my little brothers, I am so happy to share this news...hmmm...surprise...surprise...Jonnie and I have decided to get married. What better occasion than Christmas to break the news'

'What...when...?', they were kind of taken back.

I too got up... 'Sorry, it must be a big surprise to you all...we just decided it yesterday night'

'Hmm...this is so sudden...give us some time to digest this...'

We all ate breakfast silently and Abby's parents exchanged silent looks with each other and Rich and as we were helping ourselves with the second cup of coffee, Abby's father cleared his throat and started a small speech.

'Hmm...well...Abby, being the only girl in the family have had many extra privileges compared to the boys I must say. She is a fierce and an independent girl and knows what she wants. But still we were confused about her motivation and orientation all these years... Let me explain what I mean, as to her motivation, we thought she took up nursing to become a full nun later and the orientation part, she never dated much men, we wondered who does she like (meaning is she a lesbian) then she started dating you finally putting the doubt to rest....'

At this point, Abby went to sit between her parents expectantly and hugged each other in turn and then leaned on her dad...papa's girl. Her father appeared to get emotional and cleared his threat again and looked at everyone at the table and her mother as if she knew what he was going to say, and she nodded her agreement; taking the cue all brothers nodded their head making Abby beam with pleasure.

"Ah...Jonnie, if you are good for Abby, you are good for all of us...'

Everyone cheered and there was a hugging galore, everyone hugging everyone including Abby's father giving me a bear hug.

'Son, only thing that is pending...you need to formally ask me for her hand...'

I looked at Abby with a puzzled look.

'Jonnie, let me explain...', Abby came to stand beside me.

'As per Christian custom, the prospective groom asks the father of the bride the hand of his daughter in marriage. I will teach you right away, what to say and how to say...'

I was ready in two minutes and addressed her father, 'Mr. Richards, Sir. I have come to deeply love and respect Abby. Your guidance and values have shaped her into an incredible woman. I share your values and vision for a faith-based life. With your blessing, I would like permission to marry Abby and build a life honouring God together...'

Abby's father held me in a bear hug and said, 'Yes Son, you can...' in a happy thunderous voice and after nodding at her mother pulled Abby to his other side, took her hand and placed it in mine.

Everybody in a chorus chanted, 'Kiss her, kiss her...'

We kissed briefly to solemnise the acceptance, and with that public kiss, I became a complete American.

Then I was ready for the next challenge, my parents and sister. I called them in the evening, their morning nine am. I know by that time Appa would have had two cups of coffee and be in his best mood reading The Hindu.

'Appa and Amma, how are you?'

'We are fine Kanna and, how are you?'

'I am good too Appa, finished reading your newspaper...?'

'Almost, one more cup of coffee to go...before brunch'

He reads The Hindu end to end everyday and has three stainless steel tumblers (full tumbler, no half measures for him) of filter coffee before the brunch.

'Did you find any spelling mistake?'

He had been trying to spot one spelling mistake for the last 50 years after joining The Hindu as a proof reader and retiring as a Sub – Editor.

'No, it is impossible to find a spelling mistake with The Hindu because we do not commit spelling mistakes'

He was still working mentally for them even after retiring from there ten years back.

'Appa, Amma...hmm...I want tell you something'

'Yeah, tell us Kanna...what's it?'

'I am in love with somebody...ah...'

'Bagawane... that's a very good news. Who is the girl? Indian? Iyer?', that was Amma.

'Wait Ammu, let him say who...'

'Ah, well...her name Abby...Abbigail Sara Richards...American...'

'Ayyo Bagawane, Christian...', again Amma.

'So, what...white American or...'

It meant white or black, Appa was progressive but still had his own reservations proving that we Indians too are racists.

Thank God he did not know about the funky Hispanics, otherwise he would have really freaked out.

'While American Appa...'

'What is she doing?'

'She is a nurse at Chicago University Medical College Hospital and her father runs a timber business in St. Louis'

'Christian and Hindu... how will it work out? Ella acharam poche...'

'Indian culture vs American culture, will it gel?"

'What will the relatives say or how they will react?'

'Will the children be Hindu or Christian?'

'Will the children look white or brown?'

'How will we adjust to her? Will she adjust to her?'

I listened to all the queries, volleys including from my sister and brother in law.

'How will my in laws and relatives react to you marrying a Christian girl...?', my sister.

'That's why we wanted him to get married to Teju...', my Athimber.

I was spared by Teju, small mercies, as she had already got married to a software Engineer from Infosys an upcoming Indian IT company last year and settled in Bangalore.

'Can you still light deepam at home and recite Lalitha Sahasharanamam...?'

I listened to all of this and then decided to make my stand clear.

'The crux of the matter is we love each other. We have been dating for two years and decided to get married. Whether she is a Christian or American does not matter but what matters is she is good human being, caring...by the way she is a nurse, so you can understand her concern for fellow human beings...'

To tell you the truth, she does not practice religion like most Americans and does not mind me following my religion, she even accompanied me to the Perumal temple in Chicago every time I went there, just because she loves me. And more importantly I love her too.

What if I fell in love with a non-brahmin Hindu girl in Chennai itself? Or a Christian girl or Muslim girl or Jain girls?

Life would be still be different.

So, me falling in love with Abby in America is no different. We love each other and want to get married with your permission'

'How about your Abby's parents? Have they agreed?'

'Yes, they agreed just this morning. We are here at their place for Christmas'

'Oh, you are celebrating Christmas? Will she celebrate Deepavali?'

'Yes, we already celebrated Deepavali this year, I even taught her how to light the Deepam...'

'You have an answer for everything...'

'It's simply because we love each other sincerely...'

So, it on went for a few more months and finally they agreed to talk to her on a video call.

They were stunned by how beautiful she was and the icing on the cake was Abby calling my parents, 'Uncle and Aunty'; finally, they were bowled over by her American charm and said yes.

We shared the good news with Abby's parents and brothers. They were ecstatic and we agreed that we would get married before next summer, actually twice, once in Hindu tradition and once in Christian tradition.

*

I had moved to Chicago last year after a series of convincing arguments by Abby. We have been visiting each other every month for about a year and found it tedious to manage, primarily for Abby as it was nearly impossible for her to get 2 days leave together because she was a Paediatric nurse. I used to travel to Chicago on weekends when she could not travel to New York, I could manage it and work remotely for a day or two as a Star Performer, I was given the privilege.

Three months after Y2K project was completed, Gemini Info Tech put me on a Sybase project as an Administrator, so I did not face the pressure of finding another job before my H1 B visa expired or return to India; within six months of taking up the Sybase DB Administrators job, I got a good break directly with an American MNC DB company. They had their Corporate Head Quarters in Boston but had offices in all major cities in the US including Chicago. They had no problem in acceding to my Chicago posting as Corporates in the US had leap frogged to tele commuting and remote working in the 21st Century by then. It was 2001 and I had no clue then how the technology landscape would change in the coming decade and on top of the inter linking of world economy and the World becoming flat.

I was neither a Technologist nor an Economist, so I left the predictions to the respective experts and focused on our India travel the next month. There was a ton of things to do like the usual shopping, shifting to our new 2 bedrooms flat, planning work at office during my absence etc., etc., and on top of that this was my first trip home in almost 3 years since I landed at JFK with a thud.

We finally landed in Kamaraj International Airport Chennai on the wee hours of a balmy July. As we stepped out of the airport door, the typical July heat hit us. Abby gasped and exclaimed,

'Oh, my gosh...it's fucking hot...', she was tired from the 18 hours of flying and jet lag and I knew it would happen. In fact, it was shocking to me too after the cooler and colder Chicago winds.

I quickly looked at my parents for their reaction. Appa in his typical nonchalant manner welcomed Abby.

'Welcome to Chennai Abby and India too...'

Abby recovered fast.

'Hi... I am so sorry for my outburst. Thank you Mr. Sahas...' and shook hand with my Appa and Athimber. By this time, the frown on the face of Amma and Akka disappeared and they too welcomed Abby by holding her hand and Abby hugged Akka who seemed to be taken back but managed it well.

We got into the call taxi Appa had brought and set for home at Mylapore. I could see Chennai had changed a lot, new swanky office buildings had sprung up at the same time the garbage and platform dwellers still existed. I had done extensive planning to make sure that Abby was comfortable because she was a stickler for cleanliness and orderliness and both were major problems in India. I got Appa to install split air conditioner in the hall and in one bedroom, repaired and repainted the house to receive the new 'Mattuppen'. I had packed our days in India with outstation tour as much as possible to avoid the food problem and other hiccups at a typical Iyer home.

Despite all my best efforts, this what how Abby reacted about different places and people.

'What is this stench everywhere we go?' – Chennai

'This is huge and so much of sand. Is it always crowded and dirty like this?' – Marina Beach

'Why there are so many beggars?' – almost all places

'I like these chariots, and you are saying these are 15 centuries old, unbelievable…' – Mahabalipuram

'This is a well-planned city, your capital' – New Delhi

'Taj Mahal is so magnificent. I love it. It's a wonderful expression of love'

'I love these forts, marvellous' – Agra and Jaipur

'It's fucking hot, I want a beer' – everywhere we went

'I miss my Steak' – lunch time

'This is so green and beautiful, I can live here – Ooty

After the month was over, we all boarded the flight to St. Louis, myself, Abby, Amma, Appa, Akka, my nephew and niece and Athimber. First, we got married at Abby's family church, even Akka was impressed by their hospitality and then tied the knot at Sri Venkateshwara Swami temple in Chicago. We started our beautiful wedded life with a ravishing honey moon in Hawaii.

****

SIX

Chapter 6 – All is fair in Love and Work

'Bye Jonnie, don't watch TV for too long. Sleep tight, good night', with that Abby went to the hospital for her 24-hour shift. Everyone including nurses, Interns and Junior Doctors do this 24-hour shift once a month.

It was 7PM and she would return tomorrow by 9PM. Till the time I would be alone. This has been our routine in the past two years or since the time we were married. For me, work was always general shift, with occasional travel. Abby was working all 3 shifts and managed to get her weekly offs either on Saturday or Sunday as much as possible, that meant we were together half the time, so every time we were together we tried to make it special.

We cook special food when we are together, I make Dosa and Sambar or Pulav for Abby, she used to make special pasta for me without meat, or we dine out and or watch a movie or get drunk etc., etc., Abby liked all American food, fries, steak, brisket, pulled pork, buffalo wings, pan cakes etc., so we had second small fridge to store the meat, ready to eat, cooked food etc., etc., rest of the stuff were stored in the big fridge. So, we found a mutual ground most of the time not without arguments but none of us hitting the other below the belt. We were very conscious of our ethnicity and cultural differences, religion never was a challenge as Abby, I can safely say, was a non-practitioner and neutral when came to God and she didn't mind me being the typical Hindu Brahmin. I toned down my conversation with God to a small morning prayer, a little of Lalitha Sahaskaranamam, (after all I am a Sahasharanamam), and weekend temple visit when Abby was working. I should admit, like all Indian Americans, I found the prasadam and annadanam food to be delicious.

'Jonnie, if you don't mind please stop burning the incense sticks. I am allergic to the smell'

'Jonnie, please tone down the bell sound'

'Jonnie, you always miss to load the dishwasher'

'Jonnie, my God. Stop blowing your nose like that, disgusting'

These are some cryptic comments Abby made over the course our marriage and I too had made some similar comments about her.

'Abby, stop throwing your clothes all over the place. Why don't you dump them in the washing machine directly?'

'Don't kiss me after eating Brisket. I feel like vomiting'

'Oh, you snore so much and sleep with your mouth open. Ugly'

'You shit once in two day and the toilet stinks'

These were some of the comments we made about the other person or differences, some of them could have turned nasty but we knew we were built and brought up differently, a Caucasian and an Oriental and chose to ignore it for our own good.

I was earning close to 70 grand a year and Abby made something like 40 grand and I knew it was tickling Abby to some extent but she never let it turn into jealousy.

'Jonnie, how come you Indians are so smart but why India is still not developed like Unites States?'

'Well, we are Intelligent and hardworking but we lack the discipline and let corruption rule. Plus, we were ruled by the British for over three centuries who stole trillions of dollars from India. If I try to explain in detail, it would become a major history and sociology class'

'There is a new Indian Doctor with a funny name, Soundappan, Paediatric Neuro Surgeon. I asked him does his name has any connection to sound, he said no. It is their family God I believe. He is a Tamil like you, I remember where he is from, hmm...Salem....'

'That's great, I know the City. It's a famous city called 'The Mango City' because of the tasty mangoes grown there'

'You know, he makes 300 grand a year,' this time I could feel some envy.

'Wow, that's a lot of money. I wish I could also break the 100k barrier'

'You know, you Indians are a greedy lot. He says there are Indian docs who make half mil each year'

Despite the fact that we were a couple and are earning different salaries, the entire expenses were shared equally between us. Abby, would not let me spend even a cent more just because I was earning more or I was a man. Fiercely American, all are equal and financially independent. We allowed ourselves to buy gifts for each other for occasions but paying for shopping is forbidden.

According to Abby, one is entitled for their opinion but opinionated comments and advise is a strict no-no.

'Then why is that whole Unites States is obsessed with the Opinion Polls during Presidential Elections?'

'That's the most important event in the United States and it's a collective public opinion. Not individual egotistical opinions'

We managed to circumvent the issue and arrived at ceasefire without much damage. But my tongue wagged too much on one occasion when I was drunk.

'Americans are the biggest hypocrites in the world...'

That hit Abby like a rocket.

'What non-sense Jonnie? Are you out of your mind?'

'No, I am not. Americans preach the world about Green World but it does not apply to them. See how much of paper and gas is consumed by USA and still they preach carbon tax, reduce global warming etc.,'

'And what do Indians do? Leave home country and chase money elsewhere. Defectors. How may of the Indians have come to Unites States to make a good living? Why not stay back and help build India like we Americans built Unites States?'

'That's because we are the Global Workforce. Without Indian Doctors, United States and United Kingdom would not have met their health care goals in the 1970s and 80s. Same with Middle East, without Indian labours they would not have built their country and without Indian professionals Dubai would not have a become commercial hub'

'Unites States is the Super Power and we saved the world twice during both the world wars'

'And still Indians had to rescue United States and the world from Y2K disaster...?'

The argument was heated and went too far, Abby flung the whiskey glass at me and I caught it and broke it on the floor and went out like all Indian Husbands do. I returned after a couple of hours and found the glass pieces still lying there. I slowly and carefully cleaned them. In India, the wife would have cleaned them before the husband returns home, and in United States, the husband cleans whatever time he returns home.

It took us a month to patch up.

I was watching TV after supper the next day and Abby called.

'Jonnie, my goddam car broke down. Could you pick me up please?'

'Honey, no worries. I will be there in a jiffy. Did you eat something?'

'No, I was too busy'

'No worries, I will get you the infamous Chicago Pizza'

I know she loves to eat the two-inch-thick Pizza whenever she gets out of the 24 hours shift. The craving. The hospital provided decent food but the hospital staff do not eat well because of the tight work.

I found Abby in the portico waiting for me and she was taking to a handsome Indian American in a Doctor's attire.

'Hey Jonnie, this is Doctor Sound...appan..., I told you about'

'Hello Doctor Soundappan, Janakiraman'

'Hello Jonnie, Abby tells me you are from Chennai and I am from Salem'

'Yes, and your name is very different...hmm...'

'Ha, ha, you mean funny. I was ragged in Stanley Medical College as Sound of Salem'

'Sorry, I didn't mean it otherwise...'

'No worries Jonnie. It's funny to a lot of people but the name is the male version of our family Goddess 'Choudeshwari'. Same as Chamundeswari of Mysore...'

We bid each other good night and I took Abby to her favourite Giordano Pizza restaurant and Abby ordered her favourite Pizza with half steak and half spinach. The pizza is big and one can eat only two pieces out of the six and I know from practice that she would eat the rest the next day.

We were sipping Rye whiskey and talking.

'Honey, why don't you get a new car? This Honda has outlived its life'

'I don't have enough money. I am 5k short to buy a decent sedan'

'I can give you 5K, it's not a big deal'

'No, I don't want you to pay for my car'

'Okay, okay. Use my car till you get this old warhorse fixed'

'That's a deal...I love you baby...'

I knew she was getting drunk...and I was in for demanding times back at home especially in the bed.

'Which car are you planning to buy?'

'I like this Subaru sedan, kick ass...better than Chevrolet Cruz...'

'How much is it?'

'12k and it done only 50k miles...wait till I lay my hands on it...I will beat your big, ugly Ford bitch any day...'

I like SUV and she likes sedan surprisingly.

'Oh, you have only 7k...',

I managed to save 80k in my 5 years of US of A life. I too have multiple credit cards, taken the 40k car on loan, bought a high-end Nikon SLR camera, plasma TV, home theatre etc., etc., but my Indian blood still forced me to save money. There are banks still screaming under my ear, everything from home loan to vacation loan, except toilet loan but I held myself and was determined to buy a house with my own money. Maybe after 2 or 3 years. I had started looking at life beyond my current company, I was already top draw and a high performer. I was looking for more challenges and seriously wanted to join big American MNC, way bigger than the current one.

'So, you have only 7k...'

'Yeah, dumbo...'

'I can give you 10k, you buy a car under 30k miles, so it is god for 7-8 years...'

'...you......prick...why are you throwing your money at me always?'

'...you........cunt...because you are sexy and I want to fuck you...'

Thus, goes our drunk conversations most of the time. Abby was drunk fully by the time we reached home but that did not stop her from fucking my brains out.

*

My parents were visiting us that summer and what preparations we went through.

'Abby, you know my parents can't stand meat around them. I need your understanding and cooperation please...'

'Hmm... Jonnie...I understand and appreciate what you are saying...but how I do manage...I just don't eat vegetarian...'

'I have an idea...can we clear out the small fridge...so that they don't get to feel it...'

'...then, what do I eat?'

'You can order whatever you want to eat...but eating together at the table is a challenge...'

'Ho... ho...So where will I eat then...'

'You can sit on the couch or use the bedroom...'

'This is insane...', she was getting angry.

'Abby dear...I love you...and I love them too...I am only trying to juggle between both worlds of my love'

'Oh, I don't mean any disrespect for them...and I know, how you respect my parents...'

I can see she was trying to convince herself...

'Darling, you can still cook your omelettes, pancakes...'

'Wow, that's one relief... let me manage...I know they have been so good to me when we went to India last time'

'See, you liked dosai, paniyaram, vadai...she will pamper with you all of that...'

'Oh, those were so yummy...what was the red colour accompaniment...'

'Tomato chutney...'

'Yeah, tomato chutney...I will put on weight with all the ghee she uses...'

It was settled then.

My parents stayed with us for a month. We took them to Abby's parents' place, San Francisco, Los Angeles and all the Hollywood studios. As Abby did not have much leave I took them to Niagara, New York and Washington DC. Everything went well, except for the conversation about having kids, this happened despite my coaching everyone.

Abby called Appa Sir for some reason, maybe because I called her father 'Sir' and she called Amma aunty, Abby calling Amma aunty was the 8th wonder according to me.

And the fateful conversation came up one evening after dinner.

'Abby and Jonnie, I am just asking...when are you people planning to have a kid?', this was Appa.

'Appa, we have not still thought about it...'

'You are already 33, I think Abby is also 30...you should plan a kid soon...' this was Amma.

'Well...aunty... I want become a Senior Nurse in about two years, for that I need to do a two years advanced nursing course...'

'That's very good Abby, then you do it... and which college?'

'I can study at my hospital college itself...but the challenge is it would cost $ 20,000...'

Appa looked at me, I know what was coming.

'Jonnie, you have enough savings. Why don't pay her tuition fees?'

I can see that Abby was getting restless.

'No Sir, I don't want Jonnie to pay for it. If I wanted, I could have taken the money from my parents too. But I want to support myself...'

'Ah...husband paying for the spouse's education or other needs is an accepted practice in India...'

'Sir, this is America and I am an American and I do not follow Indian practices....'

I jumped in.

'Appa, she is correct and moreover for admission she requires her HOD's sponsorship...and she will get that too soon...'

I looked at Abby to say, cool down baby....and she realized that she went a bit far...

'I am sorry Sir, I didn't mean to disrespect Indian custom or you folks...'

'No need to apologize Abby, it is your career and you need to decide. We are there to help whenever you need, that's all I am saying...'

'Thank you so much Sir, I appreciate it very much'

Rest of their stay went without much issues and they left for India as per their schedule.

*

I got my big break soon with a bigger American MNC, it was a Managerial cum Architect position with 100K + salary. They wanted me to relocate to Austin, Texas, their Global Corporate Head Quarters.

I was over the moon, but little did I realize that it would become a tornado in my life and swing our marriage upside down.

******

SEVEN

Chapter 7 – The Split

"Jonnie, I can't move to Austin with you..."

The reaction from Abby was very vehement and hostile. I was shell shocked...I never expected Abby to react so badly.

'Abby...what...what the hell are you saying?...you can't move with me to Austin...'

'No...I can't. I can't move to Austin or anywhere...

'Oh my God, why can't you? Don't you love me?'

'I love you Jonnie...well, I could have moved to New York three years back itself...but I didn't...because my life is here...in Chicago...here in UChicago Medical Hospital'

'Gosh...I moved to Chicago for you. You can move to Austin for me. Your life will not end with UChicago Medical Hospital...'

'I dunno Jonnie...'

'Abby, we are married and love each other. It's only fair for me to ask. Now I've got a great job that pays 100k+...that's is enough for both us...that too with the Number One ERP company in the world...'

'Yeah, it's a great job, 100k+ salary...Numero Uno...bla...bla...you prefer that to me and that's what you have been chasing all these days while married to me...'

'No, Abby...that's not true...it's a great opportunity is all I am saying...I love you so much...it's a Managerial role...many of my friends have already become either Architects or Managers...'

'Huh...you Indians always compare yourself with others...right...and get into the rat race...and don't bother about others'

'In the corporate world one has to grow steadily...otherwise can get stuck badly...'

'If your career is important to you, my career too is important for me...'

'I can't believe what I am hearing...you can get a job in Austin...there are many big hospitals there too...'

'No Jonnie...my career is here in Chicago...'

'You sound absolutely ridiculous...Abby...and senseless'

'I can't start all over in Austin about my Advanced Nursing course, I have been working on it for five years... and now Doctor Sounds had already approved by application. I can start part time this fall...'

'I can get you admitted for 2 years full time course in Austin if you want, you don't need to work. I will take care of you...your fees...whatever...'

'Jonnie, you don't get it...do you...Fuck, I don't want to be dependent on you or anyone...'

'I am your husband, I love you, I care for you. It's my duty to take care for you, and vice versa...'

'I love you too. If you can take care of me, so can my parents. But it's not appropriate and I can't accept it'

'Fuck...you are saying it's un American to count on your husband...'

'I don't know whether or nor it is un American but it is the way I am'

'Abby, you are unreasonable. I have been of dreaming of bigger and better days for us...not just for me...we can buy a big country house with 5 bedrooms and set up the bar and home theatre in the basement; and set up your favourite barbeque at the back...'

'Ah...you can still work from Chicago, ask them you know...huh...'

'No, they made it very clear. This is a Corporate Role and I need to be based out of Austin for at least 2 to 3 years before moving anywhere in the world'

'I can't think of living anywhere other than Chicago...I studied in the Nursing School herein the Chicago University and after graduating joined the same Hospital. I have been here for more than decade...'

'What it is with you Americans...huh...that you don't move cities or states...get stuck in the same old goddamn place...'

'Dammit, that's not right, I moved from St. Louis to Chicago already'

I got so angry and stormed out of the house taking the house key and went to the neighbourhood bar and got pitch drunk.

My notice period was three months, and in a way I was hopeful that I could change Abby's mind by the time.

*

I went to Austin alone. Abby refused to accompany me as she was waiting for the Advanced Nursing Course admission. She provided me one solace if her admission does not come through she might consider resigning from her job and join me. One may call it as ungentlemanly but for my own sake and our sake, I prayed that her admission does not come through. I was not ready to lose her. I still loved her and she too loved me.

Our relationship was never the same after that fateful night's fight. We were cold to each other sometimes and warm sometimes but it did not thaw to the level where we got drunk as before or made love. We acknowledged each other at home, that's all.

My company had booked me in Hyatt Regency, full five-star hotel for a month till I found my own flat. I joined the company on the appointed date and received my IBM ThinkPad laptop and email ID etc., etc., on day one itself and so was brought up to speed. New company and new city, soon the excitement took over me. There was a lot to do in the first few weeks, formal induction for Managers (being a Manager in an American MNC is a very responsible leadership position), it comes with the perks and pressure too to deliver, both equally. I met a whole lot of people, several in the training and others at work, did a lot of other Education including self-paced ones to show me the Big Corporate way of life.

I had a team of 12 people, all smart Engineers who have been with the company for sometime and my team had 7 women and 5 men and of different ethnicity, white Americans, black Americans, Hispanics and Indians too.

My Manger who was VP took me out for lunch with the team. I did the same thing with my team as an ice breaker and we all went for lunch. Despite my insisting that it would be my treat, all of them turned it down and treated me instead. That was a good start. I spent time with them individually, understood their work, challenges and necessary personal information and told them that I practice open door policy, and they can come to my cubicle anytime or ping me on internal messaging tool and I would respond immediately. Then I worked out a few ground rules as to how we would work a as team and become a High Performing Team. The term got them excited and I was happy. Job well starred is half completed.

I started to like Austin for its quintessential Texan spirit and the warm weather, more people on the roads, great neighbour hoods where you bump into many people in a day and the never say die Texan spirit, even though I found them a bit brash but could not fault their good intentions.

Austin invariably had the aura of being the state capital, and had several big museums, bars, big music scene while the city's slogan promotes Austin as 'The Live Music Capital of the World'. I liked it there very much.

I had to plunge into my project that was to build a new RDMS Architecture for our ERP system upgrade. Obviously, I didn't get time to go to Chicago for 3 months even though we were talking on phone or texting; and the independent and self-believing Abby did not visit me too. Maybe she wanted to test, whether I am coming back for her or not or how soon.

I went to Chicago for a weekend. She managed weekly off on Saturday and we spent the time together, and went for dinner by the Riverside because that is a beautiful place and we liked the chilly wind blowing especially in the evening and always enjoyed it by cuddling each other; the Abby's favourite Pizza Restaurant was right there. I made a booking for us at 7PM. The idea was to see if we can find some of our mojo and affection in that ambience.

We were seated in the open area over looking the river. We ordered Abby's favourite steak and spinach pizza and wine for both us. Chicago Pizza in 2002 itself was costing $30 in that restaurant while outside it was $ 15 and in Austin the regular pizza was $ 5. I wanted no stone unturned in getting back Abby and avoided any talks of her moving to Austin.

'Looks like you are liking it there in Austin?'

'Yep, I like it. It's different from Chicago, while Chicago is classic Austin is both modern and rusty, the typical Texas'

'Hmm... how is the new house?'

'Oh, its beautiful. You have seen the pictures but you need to see it in person. A regular 3-bedroom house with more windows than the Chicago houses that brings a lot of warmth mainly because of the weather'

'Is it too hot there?'

'Right now, yes because of summer, 100-degree F. You need to cover your head while going out and stay hydrated. Like all of Texas, it has sun 300 days in a year...'

'How do you manage?'

'It was difficult during the first month after spending 2 years in Chicago. I am now slowly getting used it and it feels like Chennai weather. There is a connect...'

'Ah...'

I realised my mistake and changed topic.

'We are visiting your parents this Christmas as usual, right?'

'Yeah, Ricky is getting married during X mas...'

'Wow, great news. Why didn't you tell me before?'

'Ah...it was finalised only last week and you are anyway coming this week, thought of telling you in person'

I controlled my irritation and disappointment and said nothing. Thankfully, the pizza arrived and we started eating, keeping our mouth busy with pizza than words. We ate in silence for some time and ordered more wine. As we were sipping it and taking a bite of the fully yummy pizza we kind of loosened up.

'Any news (we are not using our names anymore) about the admission?'

'It should be out in a week. I hope I get the admission, that too with scholarship'

'I wish you get it...'

I flew back to Austin on Monday morning to hit the office by 10 AM after an uneventful week and I got busy with work. I was excited because our new architecture design has been approved by the Design Board and we were to start the coding soon and that called for a party. Therefore, we hit our usual bar, atypical Texan Rodeo kind of a bar with table top dance by buxom babes, it is not pole dance kind of stuff but still erotic.

We were on our third drink and I realized I was surrounded by the ladies and the men were sitting on the opposite side by some covenant. I felt something soft entangling my left hand and realised that Gabriela had taken control of my hand. Her hand was soft as rose petals and her fingers were playing with mine and it resulted in acupressure treatment, instantly hitting the nerves at the two most critical part of the anatomy, my brain and my groin. My erection was so strong like the cantilever released from the hook.

I looked at Gabriela to understand whether or not it was real and she rolled her tongue at me (I didn't know how many of the folks noticed it) and it was real. She was massaging my hand like kneading the dough, passing milli volt of electricity all over my body, before I could react she took both our hands and put it on my pecker, with hers on it. My breath became deep and long. She rolled her hand (our hands) on my pecker from bottom to tip. My heart and pecker were trying to burst out of their enclosures. Then she changed tactics, moved our hand to her crotch. She was wearing formal blended trouser, so I could feel the warmth of the hearth and by imitating the act of picking up fries from the plate near me, she pressed her boobs on my biceps. And I could feel her hard nipples through her cotton blouse.

Then suddenly I was frightened, she was my direct report, and what was happening between us could become sexual harassment.

It was actually happening to me, but it can be turned around to portray that Gabriela was the victim then that would be the end of my career with my company. There were many sexual harassment cases are reported at workplaces across the USA and actions were taken ranging from firing the employee to compensation from one hundred thousand dollars to millions to the victim depending on how much the Johnny had in the bank, not in his jeans. The issue was becoming bigger by the day.

I was told by my mentor later who had seen it all and done it all that USA had a history of sexual harassment right from the day the slaves were brought from Africa. The masters could fuck whoever they wanted, irrespective of the Christianly virtues and got away with it in the 17th, 18th and 19th centuries. It is not that things changed in the 20th century but the practice proliferated throughout the century. When the small businesses to small offices to big offices in the 1950s flourished, the bosses had free license to fuck the women they employed. And even in professional environment and big companies, Managers behaved as if they had the license to fuck their team members depending on their orientation and carried condoms in their attaches and an invite to the weekend party by the boss means exactly that. The #me too movement would start later in 2017 by the time I would have left USA for good.

The whole thing jolted me and when I came back from the washroom I was still uncomfortable to see my seat was intact between Gabriela and Meghna as before, because nobody dare take Boss' chair for their own good and when I sat on my seat it was Erotica Act 2 with Meghna from Agra and what she did was monumental.

When we were ready to go home after paying the bill, it was Meghna who pipped Gabriela.

'Boss, I can drop you on the way. I have to pass your house'

Gabriela was disappointed but covered it well, gave me a hug and whispered in my ear,' Next time Boss' and winked at me. Meghna and I took a cab and started home; half way to my house Meghna said,

'Boss, why don't we go to me place for a coffee? It's only 9PM...'

I knew what was coming and said ok. I am a hungry guy now, Abby and I have not had sex for six months, I was ready to accept when a meal was in the offing. We spoke about this and that and reached her place. Meghna made strong Americano coffee. We sat on the couch and sipped coffee. The strong coffee had its effect, our drunkenness came down considerably after drinking a cuppa.

I took the cup to the sink following Meghna, and she suddenly reached for me and kissed me full on my mouth; I responded and grabbed her ass. They were perfectly round soft football filled with cotton wool, she started moaning and I started massaging them, and sliding my hand in her crotch and rubbing her. Big tornadoes were swirling in our heads.

Meghna's tits had amazing elasticity whichever way I patted them, the tits come back to the original position after dangling a bit with a challenging stance as if to say, 'Dare to pat me again'. I was patting them and kneading them like Atta dough, what an exhilarating feeling it was.

She had an almost pinkish brown well rounded nipples that were erect and proud. I pinched each nipple and squeezed them hard which made her squeal. She was so fair, Gabriela and she had similar complexion, a bit of yellow mixed in their complexion. I was so intoxicated in my mind and balls that I was not able to differentiate between them and realized for the first time why several clients took Meghna for a Hispanic.

Meghna took me full in her mouth and sucked it so hard and then rolled her tongue all over the shaft and then licked the phallus till my shaft shook and spewed white jelly. It was an amazing orgasm, I was surprised that I survived till then because the teasing was going on since seven pm that evening. Then she used my fingers to come.

I suddenly felt guilty and wanted to leave. Meghna was disappointed but managed to say,

'No problem Jonnie, next time...'

*

The next week was busy and it was Friday, I was reviewing the codes and was totally engrossed and did not even check my cell phone for any message. It was 5PM, I took a coffee break and while returning from the washroom checked for messages. There were twenty messages from Aby, ranging from Jonnie call when free to where are you. I called her immediately.

'Aby dear...what happened...are you alright?'

'Oh, Jonnie...'

I could feel that she was close to tears, then it stuck me.

'Is it your admission honey...you didn't get it...'

'No Jonnie, I didn't get admission with scholarship...they gave it to the so called more deserving candidates'

'Then you did get admission without scholarship...?'

'Yes, but I am not taking the seat'

'Why Aby, it has been your dream to join the course. Allow me to pay your tuition fees...'

'No Jonnie, it 40k for two years. Too much to take from you. Doctor Sounds told me I can try next year and in the meanwhile he would talk to the Dean himself'

'That's very good of Dr. Sounds. You seem very upset. I am taking the next flight to Chicago, see you soon'

I reached home before midnight. Abby was waiting for me. We hugged and kissed each other, after long time, it felt heavenly. I felt a pang of guilt too. We made love again after more than six months, it was passionate given Abby's mood. We had a good time that weekend, but the guilt of what happened between Meghna and I was playing in my mind always. As it was getting time for me leave, I became restless. Like all women, Abby too noticed it.

'What's that Jonnie...you are restless...'

I told her slowly in halting words about what transpired between Meghna and I, she was silent for a long time.

'Oh, Jonnie. You too...men...oh my God'

That hit me below the belt.

I left for the airport alone in a cab, Abby not willing to drive me. I reached the airport and was waiting for my flight and my cell phone dinged.

It was a message from Abby.

'I want out'

'What Aby, what do you want out?'

'Jonnie, I want divorce...'

******

EIGHT

Chapter 8 – Indian American

'I told you marrying an American woman will not work out for us Indians, that too Brahmins...you should have married Teju, you would have been happy with kids by now...' – Akka

'Ayyo Bagawane...my Jonnie's life has become like this...nobody in our family gets divorced ever...' – Amma

'I knew Americans are too self-centred and women all the more independent, but never anticipated this for Jonnie' - Athimber

'What went wrong between you both...I thought you too were very much in love with each other' - Appa

'How will he get married again? When will I play with my grandchildren? What kind of a woman does not like the success of the husband? What kind of woman will refuse to go with her husband? I came all the way from Kumbakonam after marriage and settled in Chennai' – Amma again

'Son, I thought you too were getting along very well until your move to Austin. I told her to move with you. But she is so stubborn and boy...you messed up...' – Abby's father

We were divorced within six months; these things are pretty fast in the USA and Abby did not want any settlement or alimony. I forcefully gave her my Ford SUV and $ 20,000. I told her to use it for her Advanced Nursing Course or spend it the way she likes. She accepted it reluctantly after a nod from their parents.

We hugged and separated.

*

I was disoriented for a month, obviously my output dropped. My Boss was very understanding, that's a very good quality about Americans, and suggested that I take a break for a week or two, get rejuvenated and come back to work.

I went to Las Vegas with Ravi and Chandran (they were happily married to Indian women and had kids; infidelity is tolerated well by Indian woman till 20th century and in 21st century most of them think their husbands are too dumb to try anything new or let alone chase women) and we had such a gala time that we forgot where we went the previous day or what we did. They both enjoyed with young Belarussian and Georgian beauties, only 100 bucks for a fuck. That was serious bang for the buck according to them. I did not feel like going near any woman for the time being.

'Machan, we should go to Nashville for two days...it will help you unwind where it all started'

'No, it will be too much of nostalgia...'

'Maybe you will stumble upon a Cathy...in exchange for Abby', and they laughed loudly enjoying their own joke.

'No way, let us go to Grand Canyon and trek'

After spending four eventful nights in Las Vegas we went trekking in Grand Canyon for three days and I returned to Austin rejuvenated.

I went back to office in high spirits and plunged into work. I was not feeling guilty anymore and sad even though it was Abby who asked for the divorce, still she steadfastly refused to move to Austin despite my pleadings; six months more for all you know, I would have asked for the divorce.

I kept myself very busy and in the next three months we delivered the whole new RDBMS architecture one month ahead of the schedule. My team and I received whole lot of accolades and I got my promotion and became a Senior Manager with 20% hike and a company leased car and a whole lot of other benefits. The next levels in my company were Director and Vice President and according to my Boss, I could be Director in two years.

Meghna moved out to a new team, in her place came Marcela another Hispanic beauty originally from Costa Rica. Another Gabriela. Equally hot, equally willing. I understood the meaning of 'One Night Stand' and repeat 'One Night Stands'.

Work was good, life was good with occasional one night stands with Gabriela and Marcela. It could have been regular, I mean weekly, but I controlled myself so that only when I was desperate, it means jerking off myself was not enough, I agreed to get laid. Bosses are laid in America, special treatment. In India they would touch your feet and gossip behind you. I bought a Cadillac top end car on company lease and Gabriela proposed to me, she wanted to marry me.

'Jonnie I want to marry you and you know we can have a lot of babies. Hispanic women are good in siring more babies and bring them up too'

In a way there is a lot of similarity between Hispanic/Spanish and Indian communities. But I turned it down as I was not ready for another serious relationship even though it was already a year since Abby and I were separated.

I spent three years plus with Oracle and was still missing something despite being Top Performer and Top Talent. I was always fascinated with MIT and Harvard and applied to both for the post-graduation program; I didn't get through Harvard as they thought I didn't have enough business exposure but MIT whole heartedly welcomed me for a Master in Computer Science and Engineering that would set my bank balance off by 60k. I quit amid a lot of protests and offers from my company but got admitted to MIT that fall.

*

Life at MIT was very different compared to my first-time college experience, here the focus was on complete learning, understand the concepts and apply them too either through laboratory experiments and or publishing technical papers. HBS and MIT had strong ties and collaboration and as a result I got to attend several Management Lectures at HBS plus Sloan School of Management.

I passed M.S., with distinction and received offer from several Bay Area companies and others, finally I decided to take the offer from a German ERP giant because of my ERP background and joined them as a Director at close to 200k package and moved to Newtown square, outskirts of the famous Philadelphia in Pennsylvania state to be based at their USA Head Quarters.

It took me three months to settle down in my new job, company and city. My job involved good amount of travel both within USA and outside and travelled to Walldorf, their global corporate headquarters, India and other countries too. My company was building their business in India, so I travelled there a couple of times and visited Chennai too.

My parents and Akka were proud of me, it had been 8 years since I set foot in US of A and I was in my mid-thirties; exactly that's is the point according to Amma.

'Jonnie, you are already thirty-six, you should get married now. Big job, good salary. Chennai girls will queue up to marry you'

'Amma, I don't want to marry now that too any Chennai girl or anyone from India..'

'Then you can find an Indian girl from America itself. Not like your Abby or Gaby...'

'Yes, it is a very good idea. There must be enough Tamil brahmins in USA', Appa too chipped in.

'Jonnie, you find yourself a nice Tamil girl, not necessarily a brahmin girl. Any Tamil girl will do...they know our culture because they are brought up in our way of life. They would be suitable for you' – Akka joined, the real influencer.

'I have heard that there are language wise Associations apart from overall India diaspora association. I remember my friend from Atlanta mentioned something like that once' - Athimber

That settled the issue.

'Your friend Chandran lives in Atlanta only, you can ask him; he can tell you about it and even take you there' – Amma

'Fantastic, I think that's what you should do Jonnie' – Appa

They were deciding things for me, I don't blame them. They are only being weary and anxious because of my first marriage.

'Mama, where will be the wedding, India or US?' – My nephew and niece.

'You should get married in the US only, because we have not been there', they continued.

I thought the meeting was over, then came the clincher from Amma.

'Jonnie, you call Chandran and check with him now itself'

'Amma, it's midnight there. I will call him when he wakes up'

Amma came back with the entourage at 6PM IST and made me call Chandran.

'Hey bro, you are on speaker. Amma, Appa and everyone is here and they want to know if there is any Tamil Association there'

'Yes bro, there is, the biggest of all in the Unites States. It's called Greater Atlanta Tamil Association or GATA'

'Are there poojas and functions organized there?'

'Of course, every month there is a daylong function on the last Saturday and the festivals are bigger and better than India'

'Oh, my Sivane...do girls attend these gatherings...'

'Yes Amma, there are so many girls there to the extent Shanthi tells me to stop my 'Jollu'...'

Everybody had a hearty laugh except me because I was being set up.

'What kind of girls? Do they speak Tamil?'

'Amma, if you are looking for a match for Jonnie that's a great place. Beautiful girls from 15

years aged to women in early thirties are all there...apart from Mamies and patties... they don't speak Tamil generally but understand...'

'This is fantastic, can you take Jonnie take there and introduce him to people...'

'Absolutely Appa. Next time Jonnie visits Atlanta, I will take him there'

*

Amma was following up regularly to ensure that I land in Atlanta, more precisely GATA sooner; fortunately, some work came up in Atlanta within two months and I planned it in a way that I could attend the monthly GATA celebration too. Thus, I landed in GATA, sorry Atlanta to complete the task, the one given by my mother.

I dressed up in my best attire as per Chandran's advise and we went there along with his family.

'They serve the best puliyodarai and vadaam', - Chandran's wife Aruna. I could understand the motivation apart from not having to cook for a day.

The GATA venue on Atlanta's suburb was looking like a mini Tamil Nadu. People were dressed up in traditional plus western wear to demonstrate the power of USA, where anyone and any culture is accepted. There were the usual speeches of the GATA board members and multiple cultural programs from singing, dancing, drama etc., It was a good feeling to be there, and the lunch was yummy and I was getting bored after lunch irrespective of meeting several people.

'Chandran, I will carry on Bro...I don't think I will survive the whole day'

'Oh, don't do that please... else you will miss out on spectacular Bharatanatyam performances in the evening...'

It wasn't Chandran, I turend around and saw a gentleman in mid-fifties dressed up in Silk dhoti and shirt.

He smiles pleasantly and extended his hand.

'Parthasarathy Vasudevan, in short Partha'

'Hello sir, Jonnie aka Janakiraman Sahaskaranamam'

'I haven't seen you around before...are you new to Atlanta?'

'Yes, I am here on work and Chandran insisted that I stay to attend the monthly celebrations'

'Where do you live then? And what do you do?'

'I live in Newtown Square, PA and work for a German MNC as Director Software Engineering'

'That's awesome. I run my own business manufacturing aluminium cans for Coke and other products; before I forget I would insist as the Secretary of GATA that you please stay till the evening and enjoy the dances. And in the afternoon, there will be a comedy drama by Crazy Mohan to keep people from falling asleep'

I said OK and stayed. Oh, boy, it was worth it.

The dance performances started exactly at 6PM, series of them starting with kids and going up per age including 'Arangettram' of a couple of disciples. Then the MC made an enthusiastic announcement.

'Here comes the gold performance by Keerthana Parthasarathy, our own Superstar of GATA...she will be playing Radha yearning for the love of Lord Krishna. The announcement was followed by a thunderous applause and then entered the Apsara.

OMG, my heart skipped a beat.

She was strikingly beautiful, clad in light blue Kanjeevaram Silk saree with matching blouse and appropriate ornaments apart from big dancing bells around her ankle. Then she started her performance by bowing to the audience and then standing in a bow position sideways and opened her eyes widely and let them swirl over the audience sending one thousand arrows from Kama straight into my heart.

It was a spell binding performance and love at first sight. She was tall and lean, looked like a mix of Hema Malini and Trisha and she had round breasts that can still be seen inside thick silk blouse, and her legs were long and strong and her sinews were stretching. It was an hour-long performance with 10 minutes break in between and it felt like only 10 minutes to me.

'Machi, is that all? The performance is over...?', I asked Chandran.

'Anna, enna innnum jollu vidanuma...?' – Aruna

'Kutralam water falls was over flowing...' - Chandran

They had a hearty laugh at my expense and I was feeling so shy and buried my face in my hands.

'Hello Jonnie, did you enjoy the performance?'

I was jolted to see Mr. Parthasarathy standing next to me with a beaming face.

'Oh, Mr. Parthasarathy, it was a spell bound performance and thanks for recommending', and then it dawned on me.

'Is she your...?'

'Yes, she is my daughter. Keethu...she did her one-year Executive Program at Harvard Business School...come on let us move the cocktail area. She will join us after changing'

West meets East.

We moved to the cocktail area and picked up our drinks. We met the whole family, Parthasarathy's wife and second daughter.

'How long have you been in the United States?'

'Over eight years Sir, it includes two years in MIT and three years with my current company'

'And I work for Coca Cola as an IT Manager,' Chandran chipped in after being neglected all this while.

'Where are from originally?'

'Chennai, born and brought up there including schooling and engineering'

'I am from Palakkad and moved here 30 years back and my wife Shyamala is from Tirunelveli and moved with me; Keethu and Sandhya were born and brought up in United States. We are Indian Americans and they think they are Americans...'he laughed heartily.

We could make out that he doted his daughters.

'Jonnie, it is good to see a lot of Engineers coming from India to United States. During my time, it was all Doctors migrating to the United States and I was the odd man out'

I was beginning to wonder why he was taking so much interest in me. I exchanged a quizzing glance at Chandran and he shrugged his shoulders as if he didn't know and we found out soon.

'Hey Dad...' and she flung herself at Parthasarathy, he kissed her affectionately on her cheeks, she repeated it on all three of them.

'Hey Keethu, I want you to meet somebody...This is Jonnie...'

'Hey...'

'Hey...Keerthana...Keethu...'

'I know, I am Jonnie aka Janakiraman Sahaskaranamam, your Dad made me watch your performance, otherwise I would have long gone and it was worth. What a performance'

'Thank you Jonnie..." that was said very gracefully.

'I understand that you went to HBS...'

'Ah, It's nothing. Daddy sponsored me and gave me a fancy title VP – PR at his company. My job is to shake hands, smile and pose for the photos', she waved her hand in a dismissive gesture.

'Sorry...I didn't mean to...'

'It's ok...' I was able speak only in monosyllable, smitten by her beauty and poise.

They way her lips were moving and gesticulations and the hair dangling were shaking my heart. In a simple T shirt and Jeans, she looked like a model, all American now, and on the stage in her Bharatanatyam attire looked like Goddess Lakshmi, all Indian. Contradiction to the core. I was very confused and getting attracted to her by the second.

'It's Sandy who is the real champ, she went to MIT and is VP Manufacturing...she does all real work'

'Wow, great. I too went to MIT...'

Partha took everyone away from us to give us room.

'What are you drinking...?' all lullaby American accent.

'Singleton, single malt...'

'Good, I too will have the same'

We went to the bar together, I led her by holding her upper arm and she gave such a charming smile that made my legs loose like a drug addict's.

'Your dance performance was awesome, out of the world'

'Oh, thank you so much...I have been dancing since I was eight years...hmm...that makes it twenty-two years on the trot, dad's dream...'

Dad's girl.

'Awesome, you can go pro...'

'No, this is more of a passion and also a very good exercise'

We spoke about a whole lot of things on our own, it appeared that the world made it by design that we meet and when we were about to re-join the group, I then blurted out.

'I would like to take you out...'

She appeared shocked for a moment but concealed it well with a smile, looked at me for a long minute and said in a husky voice,

'When?'

'Hmm...next...ah...tomorrow...'

'Sure thing...'

****

NINE

Chapter 9 – Once bitten, twice joy

We dated for a year. Keethu was not the type to jump into bed on the very first date like other American women, essentially Indian in that aspect, and it was not that she was a virgin. Being a virgin at 30 means, there is something seriously wrong with the person either psychologically or the sexual orientation. I am not an expert to know if a lesbian woman not penetrated by a man is still a virgin or not.

I went back five years in time and repeated the same routine I followed with Abby, New York to Chicago and now between Philly and Atlanta with Keethu. I came to Atlanta once a month during the weekend, Friday evening, and was always picked up my Keethu in her Porsche car; rich dad, rich daughter. We used to have the best meal in town with the best wine and she never even once allowed me to pay, always settled the check by herself. If I protest, I get the standard answer, 'Daddy's orders...' as if he was the Supreme Court Judge. But when she came to Newtown Square, she always stayed with me (except for the first time when she stayed at the Sheraton) and I paid for everything. When I asked her about this out of surprise, the answer was the same, 'Daddy's order'.

Our routine was on the first day after supper Keethu took me to their grand mansion spread over 4 acres, they even had horses and stables; and I would be dropped back at Chandran's house around midnight. Next day by 12 noon the chauffeur would pick me up for lunch, I protested and protested but Partha will not have any of it. On Saturday nights, we partied till two am in a club and returned to

Partha's home.

Surprisingly, we slept together for the first time at her place, after a long Saturday night's party; after that it became a routine that I always stayed at their house. It dawned on me only after a year that they have taken me for a provisional son in law. So dumb of me.

Chandran and Aruna were constantly pulling my leg, 'Veettu Mappillai...'

Keethu's house was modern 8-bedroom mansion, big garden, garage to park 6 cars and her room itself was half my house. But she never complained about it whenever she came over. My bedroom was 500 square feet, one fourth of the house, and I guess my double king size bed compensated for it. I tried to bring a personal touch to everything, mix of American and Indian way, like cooking for her, keeping a rose for her at home, pampering her like the way the Indian boyfriends do. I didn't do barbeque because that was never my forte and I did not try to fake it. Maybe, I was trying to imitate Partha and realized that I too was doting her.

Keethu was everything; beautiful, intelligent, spoilt; half Indian but American.

I took her to my office with my Boss' permission during one of her visits; Oh boy, she was mighty impressed. Keethu noticed everything from the doorman wishing me, 'Good Morning Jonnie Sir', to white Americans treating me with deference and Hispanic, Blacks and Indians treating me with reverence.

My Boss Keith joined us for coffee at the cafeteria and it was an honour. He stayed for a while and made my day and went back to his cabin with the parting shot, 'He is a fine bloke, take care of him...'

She was astonished.

'That's what Dad told me the day when we first met...'

'Gosh, what did he say...?'

'Same thing, Jonnie is a fine bloke. Accept the date if he ever asks you'

'He said that...I can't believe it. He met me for the first time and that too only for a couple of hours...'

'Dad...is a fine judge of people. He needs only ten minutes to make his impression and he is always correct'

'Is that why he asked you to stay with me always whenever you visited Newtown Square?'

'Not exactly, he said if you expect him to stay at our house, you should stay at his'

'Really?'

'Yep, the best part was reading my mind... and he told me after my second visit to your house...Dear, if you wanna marry Jonnie...you have my blessings...'

And that's how we got married.

*

It was a grand wedding and it happened at GATA and in such a scale that people compared it to one of their grand annual days. I had my entire immediate family of 30 people flown from India to grace the occasion, my parents, Akka and family, Athimber's parents, my uncles, aunts and cousins. Partha gracefully accommodated them all near GATA for a week and kept them entertained.

Amma and Appa were over the moon for various reasons. First, their new sambandhi was a multi-millionaire, second they too are Tamil brahmins, third, their old sambandhi (Akka's in laws) were mighty impressed and were in awe of the whole thing. They concluded that their old sambandhi now would dare not trouble Akka henceforth.

A lot of my colleagues from my previous companies attended the marriage including my boss and my friends, old and new like Dave, Derrick, Ravi, Chandran, Meghna, Gaby etc., etc.,.

Three months after marriage I took transfer to Atlanta and I bought my first house, a 5 bedroom one with three thousand square feet of build up area and four thousand square feet of lawn and a garage and came with fully furnished basement including a bar counter. It was about 20 minutes' drive to my office and Partha's house albeit in different directions. We furnished the bar with all types of alcohol from wine, brandy, single malt, blended and bourbon whiskies, beer, Setzer etc., and set up a home theatre comprising of 40" Sony Plasma TV and 400W, 5.1 sound system. And we celebrated our second honey moon there, after the first one in Switzerland sponsored by Partha.

*

We settled in Atlanta. Life was good. I was busy with my work, traveling across Unites States regularly. Keethu was keeping up with her VP – PR position and living with their parents when I was away. I had no problem with them, what's the point in living alone while the hubby is away at work and when your parents live in the same city.

Life was good.

I had a great job that I enjoyed and had a beautiful Indian American wife and millionaire in laws who adored me. They expected us to be at their home every weekend. I did not mind it initially, it was a great place to wind up after a long and busy week, I drove down straight from office around five pm on Fridays and their chauffeur picked me up from Atlanta airport in case I was traveling. Keethu had bought one week's new clothes for me including innerwear and stored them in our allotted bed room.

'Keethu, why you have to buy all these? We could have brought my dress from our home'

'No, my dear hubby deserves new set of clothes when visiting their beloved in laws' place'

'Oh, how much did you blow up?'

'No Jonnie, I did not blow up any money; only spent five k for my dearest hubby'

'Daddy's order, I suppose'

'No, your lovely wife's show of affection for you'

'So, what do you want from me honey?', I asked in a mischievous tone.

'For now, a French kiss would do...'

We kissed passionately and freshened up and joined everyone for supper at six thirty pm at the barbeque, for a change it was a barbeque of exotic vegetables and fruits including avocado. We had best of the wine and supper, coffee and later single malt or bourbon whiskey in that order. Most of our weekends were spent at Partha's place except the weeks I was tired and wanted to spend time at home all by ourselves. Keethu understood initially.

I was inducted into the Atlanta high society properly by Partha. They took me everywhere, we watched a Shakespeare drama at the infamous Fox Theatre, watched American soccer football at the most acclaimed Georgia Dome, had a personal guided tour of Coca Cola centre thanks to Partha; even though I was not a fan of coke, the facility and tour was mind boggling, I was bowled over.

I realized after a year of marrying Keethu and living in Atlanta, the real meaning of what people say as 'Time Flies'. I was busy with my work during weekdays and Keethu with her part time VP – PR responsibilities and social engagements. She was a socialite and a fashionista, she attended events and balls regularly, in the afternoon and evenings and those evenings I spent time myself at home. She would tell me her program for the day, everyday morning when I was going to the office.

'I have a PR event to attend this evening along with Coke folks, will go home with Daddy...'

'I have a lunch meeting today, see you in the evening'

'I have a ball to attend this evening, do you want to join...?'

She even attended a party thrown by Paris Hilton, I could not attend it as I was traveling; some days when Keethu did not have any engagement, she would go to their parent's place.

'I going to Dad's place. Come over in the evening', she would text me often.

'No, I will be late. Are you coming home?'

'I will let you know'

Keethu was not much of a home maker thanks to the fashionista upbringing and I ended up doing all the household chores, washing the dishes/clothes, ironing, housekeeping, cooking etc., and not that I was doing everything by my own hands. We had all kind of appliances at home, courtesy Partha, entire house revamp and all appliance like microwave, dishwasher, cook top, chimney, vacuum cleaner, refrigerator, deep freezer etc., etc.,

I was getting tired of the household chores myself and hired a Mexican lady as a house keeper, she would come for two hours in the morning and two hours in the evening and do the day's chores. She would cook rice and nice Mexican chipotle dishes too whenever I wanted.

Keethu took me to a charity ball once, I was not keen in attending such grand social functions as I found such events as phoney and people put on an act, typical American. This was a charity event to collect money for a cancer foundation but nobody knows where the money goes and how it is spent would be anybody's guess, same like India. I guess it is the same in all countries. The event was seriously high profile, attended by the who's and who of Atlanta including Partha and hosted by someone similar to Oprah Winfrey's stature.

Keethu was one of the hostesses and was busy engaging the 250 people who had gathered for the $1000 dinner and were expected to donate more. She introduced me to several people,

'Hey, this is Jonnie. My husband, he is a Vice President with...'

They collected roughly $ 2M, that's big money. We left the hotel around 10PM and I was tired.

'Baby, did you like it?'

'Yeah, too hi-fi for my likes?'

'But these people are the power house of Atlanta, knowing them would help you in some way'

'I don't how it would help me with my annual performance appraisal' I said with a smile.

'I get it... sometime you can be sarcastic'

'No darling, I am telling you what I feel openly'

'I know you always speak your heart'

'Speaking of the heart, I am missing my sweet heart half the time'

'Oh, you know Jonnie...the high life demands me to do this, do that, be there etc., etc.,'

'I am not complaining but you can come home and be with me. Need not sleep at your parents' place all the time'

'I will try to be home with you honey hereafter…'

*

We had our first row soon after that.

For three months, things went well. I could see Keethu made real effort to come home after her engagements.

'Honey, I will be home for after dinner'

'Dear hubby, I will be home before you. I will cook dinner for you'

'Sorry honey, it will be too late, I will go to Appa's place tonight'

She was home most of the days and I cooked dinner with the help of Rosaline, our Mexican maid; some days I made South Indian dishes including rice, sambar and Rasam and some days Rosaline would make Mexican dishes and chicken for Keethu. She eats meat once in a while at home and regularly outside, chicken and sea food. No pork or beef.

One day evening she messaged me, 'Honey, I will be home for dinner'

So, I teamed up with Rosaline and cooked Mexican rice and vegetables for me and Chicken Stroganoff for Keethu and we kept the dinner ready at the table by 630PM and I waited for Keethu.

It was already seven pm.

'Honey, I am stuck in a discussion, a bit delayed. Sorry see you soon'

I waited for thirty more minutes, Keethu did not come home. I thought she was on the way.

I poured myself a drink and sat down to watch CNN and I got engrossed in the news and didn't notice that it was already eight pm.

'Darling, I am waiting. Where are you?'

I didn't get a message for ten minutes and called her. She didn't pick up. I messaged her again.

'Keethu, what time you will be home?'

'Honey, the meeting is still on. I will come home as soon as it finishes'

I know what these meetings are, they are some mostly high-level gossip and politics and how much money to collect in the so-called social gatherings.

I was hungry and had my dinner.

'Keethu, I had my dinner. Let me know whether or not you are coming for dinner'

'Sorry honey. I am stuck. I will come late...'

I was so angry that I wanted to throw the Chicken Stroganoff into the dust bin, controlled my anger and put it in the fridge. I could not sleep, poured myself a drink and sat down to watch TV.

Time was ten pm. No sign of Keethu.

Time was eleven pm. No sign of Keethu.

It was almost midnight and Keethu reached home finally and she was drunk.

'Oh, honey...you...are still awake...'

'I am waiting for you. Where did you go?'

'Sorry Jonnie, Martha joined late...and you know she is a big shot...'

'So...'

'She wanted all of us to go for a drink...and so we went'

'Martha asked you and went...here I have been waiting for you and did not think of me'

'I am so sorry...', she came to hug me but I pushed her away.

'I am getting tired of your behaviour Keethu, ignoring me and home'

'What do you mean? Do I have to spend all my time with you? Or wait for you at home like all other wives?'

'What all your time? You are hardly spending any time with me...we have been married for a year now. I thought you would change a bit for me but you did not change at all'

'Why should I change myself for you? I have own way of life'

'It is part of the institution called marriage, both husband and wife change to accept and accommodate each other. I did change myself for you. So, expecting you to change for my love, is it so hard?'

'Why are you arguing so much Jonnie?'

'Am I arguing? You promised to come home on time and regularly and managed to do it only for a month or two and you are back to your old routine. Socialise...party every day...come home late or go to your parents place'

'What nonsense? Am I supposed to give up my personal life for you?'

'If we can't adjust our personal life for each other, what is the point in getting married?'

'I don't know, I can't be a house wife like everybody else'

'I am not asking you to be a house wife but asking you to be a good wife...If this is too much to ask I don't know...'

I went into the bedroom to sleep and Keethu did not follow me. We slept separately in two different rooms that night and didn't speak to each other for a week.

*

It was a Friday evening, I was ready to leave office and my phone rang. It was Keethu.

'Hey Jonnie...'

'Hey Keethu...'

We became normal after a week when Keethu said sorry again. I immediately adopted 'Forgive and Forget' policy.

'Appa wants us to spend time with them this weekend'

I realized that we have not been to Partha's house together in a month.

'Oh, that will be good. I can go there straight from office. And where are you?'

'I am in the office, I will go with Appa'

'Cool, see you soon'

In fact, it was good to be there after a month. It became clear to me more than year after marrying Keethu that they wanted me to stay with them, 'Veettu Mappillai', so ignorant of me. Now I could realise Partha's disappointment when I bought my own house in Atlanta but gracefully hid it.

'Hey Jonnie, long time...'

'Hey Partha, yeah. Work has been hectic and I was traveling too'

I could see that both Keethu's mother and sister too were happy to see me. We all had dinner amidst a lot of banter and laughter.

Partha caught up with me alone while we were having the drinks after dinner.

'Keethu feels bad about letting you down...'

I frowned, did Keethu talk to his Appa about what happened between us. Not good. Partha was quick to add,

'No, we didn't talk about. She only said that she stood you up and you got angry. That's all and she will not let that happen again'

I nodded and passed on to other topics and retired to our respective bedrooms. Both Keethu and I were in good mood and had intimate sex that felt good. I have been thinking about having a baby for some time, thought it would be the right time to bring it up with Keethu.

'Keethu...'

'Hmm...', she was in a dreamy mood.

'I am going to be thirty-seven soon...'

'So what?'

'You will be thirty-two soon...'

'Since when you are tracking my age?'

'Not from that perspective. I was thinking we have been married for close to two years now, precisely eighteen months...I think we should start a family...'

'What family?'

'I am ready to be a father. I think it is time we plan for a baby'

'Oh, no. Me, mother...no...I don't want to be a mother...'

****

TEN

Chapter 10 – The inevitable

I was disappointed.

'Why Keethu, you don't want to have a kid...and you don't want to be a mother...'

'No Jonnie. I think I am not cut out to be a mother'

'It is just a mind sent. Imagine holding the bundle of joy in your hand'

'No, I am not able to imagine that. I never considered myself a mother'

'Is this feeling for now or forever...?'

'I don't know, I can't change the diapers, or feed the baby or don't know how to manage if the baby cries...'

'One can always learn it and parenting is a joint responsibility', with that I dropped the discussion for the time being, did not want it to become an argument.

We went about our routine for a month as usual. My mind was coming back to fatherhood again and again for a reason, it was summer and everywhere we went we ran into families with kids from new born to toddlers to boys and girls. I was envious whenever I saw a father playing with the kids and Amma's regular enquiry too did not help it either.

'Jonnie Kanna, when are you planning for a kid?'

'We are talking about it Amma, we will plan soon'

'And I want to play with my grandson Kanna...'

'Sure Amma, you can come to United States whenever you want once we have the baby. But for now, please be patient'

There was another event that made my longing stronger. That was Vandana, Keethu's sister's wedding. Vandana had been dating Patrick for two years and she was three months pregnant. Patrick was working for Coca Cola in their Procurement Department and that is how they had met. Partha arranged for a hurried marriage, in GATA itself, but no less grand than ours. I got Amma and Appa to take the next flight to attend the marriage.

'How is this possible? That she is three months pregnant? What upbringing is this?'

'Amma, this United States. It's a free country and it is common to have children without marriage'

'Ayyo Bagawane...what kind of family will it be? What do the kids call them, 'Amma, Appa...' or something else?'

'What else Dad and Mummy only?'

'Oh, and when are you going to have children? You and Keethu have been married for almost two years now'

'Soon Amma...'

Sandhya and Patrick went to Paris to celebrate their official honeymoon and Partha took us to Bahamas for a week. What a place! So serene and so beautiful, turquoise blue waters and sandy beaches and more than three thousand islands. We stayed at Grand Hyatt in Nassau and did all the things the tourists are supposed to do, scuba diving, yachting and partying on the beach bars etc., etc., Everything was expensive except sea food and sea related stuff because everything else was imported.

Keethu and I were relaxed and warmed up to each other because of the location and holiday mood. We played with each other like we always did and went into sex overdrive. We landed back in Atlanta rejuvenated after blowing up ten thousand dollars thanks to Partha.

I plunged back into work after the break and time flew past. I was busy at work when I got Keethu's call.

'Jonnie...'

I could sense something wrong in her voice.

'What happened Keethu?', I was alarmed.

'I missed my period'

I missed my heartbeat. But recovered fast not to reveal my joy.

'What? How many days?'

'Almost six weeks'

'Oh, you didn't notice all this while'

'I don't know, somehow missed it'

'Maybe it is delayed. Do you feel uncomfortable? Vomiting, backache or any other problem..'

'No, I am feeling a bit uneasy from the morning'

'It's nothing to worry, why don't you meet the Doctor if you want?'

'No, I don't think so. I will go to Appa's place, you come over there'

I was elated, finally my dream of becoming a father is about to come true. I finished work early and reached Partha's house with a lot of happiness and anticipation but when I reached there, I felt something was amiss.

Partha and Keethu's Amma were sitting in the living room with a worried look on their face.

'Anything wrong Partha? Where is Keethu?'

'Ah, she is in her room'

'Is she ok?'

'Yeah, she is good...'

'Then why are you looking troubled...'

'Let us wait for Keethu'

Keethu came in to the living with puffed eyes.

'What happened Keethu? Are you OK?'

'No, I am not good. I don't want the baby...'

'What are you blabbering Keethu?' – Partha

'Are you crazy?' – Keethu's Amma

I can't believe what I was hearing. I thought Keethu would come around over a period of time but this was too much for me hear.

'What do you mean you don't want the baby? You didn't even go to the Doctor'

'But I tested, it came positive'

'Let us first visit the Doctor and get the confirmation' – Partha.

For the time being, the cyclone was averted but my mind was in a turmoil. How to convince Keethu? How to make her understand that motherhood is the most beautiful thing in life and the biggest gift one can get.

Next day morning, I took her to the Doctor. After the check-up and USG scan the Doctor confirmed her pregnancy, in its seventh week, and congratulated us.

I was over the moon. Keethu was very upset and our argument started right in the car way back home.

'I don't want to keep the baby. I have told you this a million times. You still don't get it'

'Don't talk non-sense Keethu, baby is a boon. God's gift to couples and we should feel we are blessed'

'Boon, gift…I neither understand nor desire them. I can't manage a kid and I can't be a mother'

'Let's get home first and then talk it out with your parents'

Partha and Keethu's Amma were ecstatic, they even distributed sweets to everyone. I enjoyed one too followed by a strong cup of americano.

Keethu refused everything and went to her room to change and came back after half hour.

'Keethu, see Sandhya is now in her sixth month and you are in your second month. It is a moment to cherish for us as your parents' – Keethu's Amma.

I can understand the feeling, two grandchildren six months apart. What a way to celebrate even millions of dollars cannot get you such happiness.

'Trust me Keethu, life will never be the same with the kid. I can still remember carrying you the day you were born. The feeling was incomparable' – Partha.

Keethu was mentally exhausted and I sat beside her, put my hand on her back to sooth her and at the same time thinking seriously how to get her out of her current mind set. I guess Partha too had similar thoughts wondering what was wrong with their elder daughter. The younger daughter gets pregnant before marriage and the elder daughter does not want the baby after getting pregnant. What an irony!

Suddenly Keethu blurted out.

'I want to get the abortion done'

We were all shell shocked and didn't expect Keethu to be so adamant.

It was Partha who recovered first.

'Keethu darling, there is still enough time for that if that's what you want. Let us give it a few days and then circle back'

I stayed at Partha's place itself for a week and went to office from there and spent time with Keethu every day in the evening. Her vehemence had come down a bit but she had not backed down from her stand. She had gone into a shell despite Sandhya's counselling and sharing her joy of motherhood. Her parents were following the wait and watch approach and asked me to be patient. I could understand their perspective, two grandchildren six months apart.

Amma and Appa were so happy at the news, and I could not bring myself to tell them the actual problem. They would be so disappointed. I was feeling guilty about giving them false hope, what happens if Keethu goes with the abortion. I was torn by the feeling of losing God's gift. On one side, I was visualising rocking the baby in my arms and on the other side I was tormented by the abortion and missing my unborn child. Everyday was like a ticking time bomb, I did not know when Keethu would start the abortion topic again.

The time bomb exploded soon. I got a text one day while at office.

'I have aborted the child for good'

I rushed to Partha's house and it looked like a house mourning death. I have never seen Partha and Keethu Amma so sad and angry at the same time.

I was mad and shouted.

'How the hell did you do it?'

'Did the hospital not ask for my permission?'

'I went to a place where they did not'

I freaked out and left Partha's house for the last time after an hour of shouting back and forth.

And we were divorced within six months.

****

ELEVEN

Chapter 11 – Third time Lucky

I sold the Atlanta house and went back to Philly, Philadelphia not the outskirts or Newtown Square where I lived two years back. This time I wanted to live in the city and rented a two bedroom flat in downtown Philly and moved in and the only challenge was parking my big and bold Cadillac, otherwise I liked Philly's vibes. This time I really started enjoying the vibrancy of Philly, the old electric poles and the colourful facades, the most infamous Philly steak and the local neighbourhood buzz. Stepping into the Corporate Office and occupying one of prized cabins felt good, so was the corporate buzz and the camaraderie. I was missing that in Atlanta because I was very senior compared to the people working there and in the Corporate Office there are many equals and a first among the equals; and that makes it intriguing if you are in the game, it is called Rat Race. I wanted to take work seriously and life easy. So, I was getting into the Rat Race seriously now and was strengthening my position with India Delivery centre project. My parents were very upset about what happened and Akka and Athimber were very livid but let me move on with my life.

The big change I brought about was changing my eating habits too. I wanted to re born and removed my punool to start with and one day, during weekend for lunch, I went to the famous steak house and ordered a Steak, well cooked. I have seen Abby eat the steak so much so the look was not a deterrent to me. It was pink in the middle and brown at the periphery, I cut out a small piece and put in my mouth tentatively and chewed slowly; contrary to my apprehensions, it tasted good. I finished the meal with the help of pints of beer and felt good. Last one year of frustration, depression and neglection had made me a zombie of a sort and now I felt I was born again. I am a free man. I gave up all my inhibitions and felt fully liberated. I became an all cuisine eating global American not bound by my sacred thread anymore. Not wearing it, did not make me feel bad at all.

Work too became interesting as our India project was going on in full swing that required all my attention as I was the lead for that team. I travelled to Bangalore once in three months and fell in love with the city, the climate, the gardens and the cosmopolitan culture. The Indian teams were very smart and accustomed to working with Americans and Europeans, behaved like a reflection of the American team, after all Indians had been watching Hollywood movies for over forty years. My stay at Hotel Leela Palace was so lovely and peaceful, it was not a hotel but a resort or a garden right in the heart of the city. The pain was the traffic and the time it took to commute the ten-mile distance to the office and back. Weekends, I was taken for a city tour or Mysore or Coorg or Belur and Halebedu etc., by the team. The highlight was eating dosai in the infamous VV Puram Dosa street. One Masala Dosai was only thirty-five rupees, less than a dollar, so cheap and yummy. So, during weekends when I was on my own, I went out for a walk to explore the place around my hotel and eat lunch or dinner; language was a not a barrier as most of the people spoke Tamil. I had Idly vadai, dipped in sambar and filter coffee for twenty-five rupees at a nearby Udupi Park that cost me two hundred rupees in Leela Palace and Bangalore was full of such Udupi hotels. Walking on the road was a big challenge. There were no proper foot path for pedestrians, one had to wriggle through the zooming two wheelers. Even though I was born and brought up in India, the ten years of living in the United Stated had made me more disciplined thus the walking on Bangalore roads was a nightmare.

I was exploring Philly too as much for it was the capital of the United States during the civil war and after, it had a big history to it and one of the biggest cities of North America and a professional soccer team by the name Philadelphia Union of which I became a follower. I just wanted to treat Philly as my first city in the United States in a decade of living in the USA; no New York, no Chicago and no Atlanta. I liked the narrow roads and red buses and six months flew like six weeks.

One morning, I was taking out my car as usual at seven thirty am, reversing carefully to manoeuvre the Cadillac in the small parking space and heard a banging noise.

Oh, did I bang something or someone?

I got down form the car hurriedly to find a woman too get down for her car.

'Oh, I am so sorry...It was all my mistake...'

'Oh, what happened?', I was still trying to figure out what had happened.

'I was backing up too fast as I was late. Didn't see your car'

'Even I didn't see your car, I should have spotted you too...'

'No, no. It was dumb of me'

'No worries, at least it happened in the car park, not on the road. After all we are neighbours. Let us check out the damage'

I inspected the damage, it was a small bump on my bid Cadillac but a big dent on her old Honda. She was doubly upset.

'Oh my God, that will cost me dear'

I have seen her before in the apartment, living on my floor and we had bumped into each other in the lift sometimes. She appeared to be a plain woman to me earlier, now at close quarters she looked handsome and beautiful, a high-rise chin and wide lips that were curved like a question mark due to the tension. Curiosity over took me. She was dressed up in her track suits.

'Where were you going?'

'I was going to the park to run. I generally leave by 715AM to beat the traffic, today Dolly was misbehaving and I got late'

I deduced that Dolly must be her pet.

'Oh, pets can be demanding. That's why I don't have one'

'She is a darling but today something got the better of her'

'And what do you do?'

'Oh, I teach 8TH graders at the Philly Cyber Public School'

'Good Morning Teacher. I am Jonnie...Janakiraman Sahas..'

'Hey, I am Charlie, Charlotte Lidia Johnson. I think we live in the same floor'

'Of course, we have bumped into each other in the lift'

'I am so sorry again. Do we report this to the police?'

'No, no way. We are neighbours and won't do no such thing. It's all right with me. Only you have a bigger dent'

After much convincing, Charlie let me go to the office.

*

I was home in the evening, checking and replying to my emails. There was a knock on the door. I was wondering what to eat for dinner and it annoyed me. I don't get uninvited guests. I opened the door and found Charlie smiling at me.

'Hey Jonnie...sorry to intrude like this...'

'Hey...er...Charlie. No, no problem...'

'I wanted to say sorry for what I did this morning', she waved the wine bottle at me.

'Oh, so sweet. Please, come on in...'

And we toasted each other and were bantering on my couch soon. Charlie came from a family of teachers, her grandfather, father and uncles were all teachers. She was the eldest of four siblings and had bought this flat with her hard-earned money.

I took a closer look at her now. She was a big woman and gorgeous. Awesome tits and butts. I liked it that way.

We finished the bottle of wine and ordered food from outside. Charlie leant everything about me by the time we finished dinner. She was very good in gleaming in all information out of me. She knew all about Riley, Abby, Meghna, Gaby, Keethu and everything and still she did not mind a two-time divorcee in me and we made love after the first meeting. I got laid and was baptized as a true American. Finally.

*

'Charlie, I am traveling to Bangalore next week, so I will be out for two weeks including a couple of days in Chennai'

'Dear Jonnie, you are going away to Bangalore more often to my liking. Are you up to something fishy?'

'Fishy, mushy...my work is calling me. After all Bangalore is my second love'

'There, I got you..ha...ha...Why can't I go with you to Bangalore?'

'Are you serious Charlie?'

'I am, I haven't been to India or any Asian countries in my life'

'How about your school?'

'They owe me some leaves, I can take a vacation when I want it'

'Cool, I need to take my Manager's approval for taking my partner on work tour as per policy. Let me do that'

We flew into the small Bangalore International Airport from London by BA. I knew from my previous visits that Hotel Leela Palace was hardly one mile from the airport but we could not walk due to the luggage and the foreigner tag. We took a customary taxi that deposited us at Leela Palace. The front office staff were courteous enough to give us early check in. We freshened up and went down for breakfast, it was only nine am on a Sunday that meant we had to fight the jet lag till the evening and trust me it is a tough job.

Bangalore was love at first sight for Charlie.

'Wow, this city is so beautiful. Cosy weather and lullaby like monsoon drops...'

The coffee house was big and busy and lazy on that Sunday morning and the spread was outstanding. I had already warned Charlie about beef not being served at most of the restaurants so it was not a disappointment.

'Man, this coffee shop is better than the Hyatt Regency in New York', she liked the Jaipur pink influenced building and the idea of walking out of the hotel on to the road pavement that made the hotel in full harmony with the surroundings, no compound wall to separate it. After heavy breakfast and many cups of irreplaceable south India filter coffee, we heard about the Kemp Fort Big Shiva

Temple that was less than a mile away which was a big attraction with its 80 feet tall Lord Shiva's statue.

'Charlie, there is a big Hindu temple ten minutes' walk form here that has a huge Lord Shiva statue. Do you want to go there?'

'Ah, why not?'

When we reached after the shot walk we were astonished to see Lord Shiva statue from the road itself, it was magnificent and gave me good bumps.

'Gee, this is awesome. I love it,' Charlie pumped in the air.

The statue was so big, surrealistic, masculine Lord Shiva was towering over Mount Kailash in his bluish ash colour with the snake atop his neck and the half-moon on his head. Apart from the statue the rest of the temple was open on all sides, with a quadrangle in the front where devotees were sitting in silence and living in the moment.

'Jonnie, I want to pray...can I?'

I was shocked by this question from Charlie, I never expected such a question from her. From an American.

'Oh, yes you can. It's up to you, like this'

I showed her how to fold the arms in the Namaste gesture, close the eyes and pray. She prayed for one full minute to everybody's else's surprise.

'I love it here. Can we sit here...' she pointed out to the floor where people were sitting in groups, families and friends.

'Yes, we can. Before that let us go near the deity, touch his feet and come back to sit here'

All the devotees were allowed to go around the deity in the so-called open sanctum sanctorum and then touch Lord Shiva's feet and pray. The temple folks did not allow Charlie to go in there obviously assuming she is a Christian, a non-Hindu owing to her white complexion. She was disappointed. I pacified her.

'Charlie, non-Hindus are not allowed to enter The Hindu temples in general except ISKON. We can sit on the floor like you wanted'

I took her to the floor and we sat down with legs folded and watched around. The people appeared to be in a trance, many of the eyes were closed and praying, some of them meditating, some of them smiling and some of them gently chatting. We spent an hour there to my surprise and Charlie was in no mood to leave.

'Oh my God, this is so divine. I have never seen so many people visit churches back in United States...'

'Hinduism is a way of life and not just region. We pray to God ten times in a day and follow the Hinduism process all the time'

She even put Vibuthi on her fore head not only my shock but everyone around and some even commented.

'Looks like your American wife want to convert to a Hindu'

'What did she say?'

'She thinks you are my wife...' I chuckled.

'Oh, is that whet she thinks? That we could be husband and wife...Ah, why not?'

I was jolted out of my reverie. Charlie wants to get married to me? It was not even a year after separating from Keethu and I was not yet ready for another marriage. I had to divert her.

'Charlie, do you want to go the CBD of Bangalore? MG Road and Brigade road? A must see..'

'Really, let us go'

I sighed a big relief and hailed an auto. Charlie enjoyed the auto ride so much.

'This is so cool and adventurous. What's this called?'

'Auto Rikshaw, auto in short. It's a three-wheeler and the most popular ride in India'

'Awesome, I love this. Mind blowing. I see more of them on the road than buses'

'These compliment the public transportation for public mobility. In some part of the country they replace the public transportation'

We were dropped near Cauvery Handicrafts junction, the perfect place at the Brigade Road and M. G. Road junction. We walked the length and breadth of MG Road enjoying the Sunday crowd and weather. People were making serious fashion statements that was nothing short of New York. I remember loving M G Road and Brigade from my college day visits. They still had same pull on people. Then we entered Brigade Road.

'Why is this called Brigade Road?'

'There are a lot of Indian Army and Air Force establishments around this area and this is called cantonment'

'Did the Indian Army build these roads?'

'Maybe, Brigade Road used to be the place for the officers to go in the evening for entertainment with its bars and ladies those days'

'Oh, really. And did they have live bands performing?'

'I guess so until recently...'

'Wow, there a so many pubs here...Do they serve tap bear?'

'Of course. Bangalore is the Pub Capital of India. Come let's find a place of your choice'

She finally settled on a Pub in the first floor in the middle of Brigade Road and we enjoyed King Fisher Draught beer with nice chicken and mutton on the side. I can see that she was really enjoying herself...so much in contrast to Abby's first visit to India. I didn't know why I thought about it or Abby but the thought was twitching in my heart. We were so full of beer and meat and so decided to walk down to Commercial Street.

We walked down Commercial Street twice and settled down in the iconic Woody's Restaurant for their signature south Indian filter coffee. The we walked on Commercial street again and were window shopping, suddenly Charlie shouted.

'Hey, I want that dress...'

I looked at that direction and found a beautiful Salwar suit.

'What? This one? Are you serious?'

'Yeah, I am dead serious...'

We went inside the shop to find out. They did not have any size to fit Charlie and we strolled Commercial street and finally landed in a mid-sized shop. The owner was a persistent guy and he found a dazzling big size blue salwar kameez from his uncle's shop. Charlie was sizzling in that radiant blues and she insisted that she would wear that only back to the hotel and refused to change even when we went down for dinner.

We were enjoying our scotch and suddenly Charlie stood up and shouted, 'I like it here, I like India...'

Everybody in the restaurant cheered her. She sat down in her chair and leaned on me.

'I thing I want to get married to you Jonnie... and live in India...'

******

TWELVE

Chapter 12 – Bundle of Joy

'That is the second time you mentioned it today. Are you serious about getting married?'

'Of course, Jonnie. I am dead serious. And I want to get married to you...'

I was taken back. Sat there thinking.

'Hey Jonnie, you didn't respond'

I sat up and looked into her eyes and saw her eyes glowing with love and managed to say finally.

'Yes, I want to marry you too. But on one condition...'

She tilted her head as if challenging me.

'What is it?'

'I want loads of kids...'

'Hey...you got it...' she jumped to her feet and kissed me fully on my lips and shouted to everyone in the restaurant.

'Hey folks, we are going to get married...' and everybody cheered for us.

'Jonnie, I want to get married right now, right here'

'Charlie, what do you mean?'

'I want to get married in India according to the Hindu custom'

I was baffled wondering whether she was pulling a fast one on me. Her face was set in her favourite posture and pursed lips that meant she had decided.

'I want to get married right here and right now', she repeated.

I called Appa to break him the news and he hurriedly went about organizing the wedding. We reached Chennai from Bangalore on

Friday and got married on Sunday at the famous Kapaliswaran temple in Mylapore and spent our traditional first night in our house itself as per Charlie's insistence. Amma and she became too close and too fast to everybody's surprise. She stated calling Amma and Appa as such and even I was bowled over and my heart was filled with joy. For some reason, my mind raced back six years and remembered Abby's first visit to India and how different this one turned out be.

Charlie, was dressed up in 'aru gajam' kanjeevaaram madisar seelai' and me in traditional panja kashtam. My family, relatives and friends were so taken back and stated calling Charlie, 'America Mami'.

We spent our honeymoon in Fisher man's Cove in Mahabalipuram and Charlie became overnight sensation to the extent we were given a candle lit dinner free. Two days before we were to travel to the US, Charlie dropped the next bombshell.

'Jonnie, I want to extend my stay for two more weeks and visit Kanchipuram, Tanjore etc.,'

'Oh, honey. I can't take any more leave. I have been out for three weeks already'

'Not you Jonnie boy... ', she said it with a smirk, 'Only me'

'My gosh...you are going to give me heart attack at this rate. Please explain yourself'

'I will stay for two more weeks and visit all famed temples of Tamilnadu with Amma and Appa and then come to Philly'

'What about your work?'

'Oh that...as of this morning I quit'

I collapsed into the sofa.

'Making a family is my priority for now. Charlie is a woman of focus'

'Do you realize when we have kids you may not be able work again?'

'Oh, you won't take care of me and kids?'

'Arr...this sounds so surreal...you are American and you won't sit idle at home and expect your hubby to feed you...'

'I am not American anymore, I am half Indian like you are half American …I am Mrs. Charlotte Janakiraman…'

Mom was beaming with pleasure and hugged and planted a loving 'mutham' on her cheek and Appa looked stunned as if Parvati Devi had appeared in front of him.

*

I landed in Philly after strenuous travel of twenty hours and a severe jet lag. I left India on a Friday night and all three of them Appa, Amma and Charlie hired a nice cab and started on the Tamilnadu yatra on Saturday early morning itself, by the time I landed they had already visited Vayalur, Sri Rangam and Tanjore and were on the way to Kumbakonam.

On Monday morning I visited office and received a whole lot of surprise congratulations from everyone, from my Boss to peers to team members. The whole week I partied with all, first with my Boss and Peers, then with my team and others. Ravi and Chandran flew over the weekend and celebrated my new status that weekend.

'Machan, you really have some 'macham' on you? Three gorgeous wives in 10 years…we are stuck with one. Poor souls', they pulled my leg for whole two days. Mid next week I received a bunch of polaroid photos delivered by DHL express, sent by Charlie. Oh, they were so enjoyable. Charlie was an avid photographer and shoots everything that interests her, there were photos of their temple trip from the vast complex of Sri Rangam to Trichy Rock Fort, Tanjore Brahatheeswarar temple's majestic tower with the indomitable 10 ten ton stone atop the tower, innate carvings of the tower and sculptures, mindboggling Kumbakonam temples, the Oxford of the east, and the majestic Madurai temple captured in all its grandeur and the ace up the sleeve being the Pamban bridge to Rameswaram. But what really stood out were three photos, one group photo of Amma, Appa and Charlie in traditional sari and dhoti and garlands; second was Charlie drinking Kumbakonam Degree Filter coffee in a brass 'dabara set' in the local coffee shop in Kumbakonam and third drinking Jigir Danda at the local shop in Madurai.

*

As I expected, Charlie fell sick with throat infection and viral fever because of the travel. She took one week to recover, stayed at Chennai home, went to Apollo Hospital, went to Kapaliswaran temple once recovered etc., etc., all these and more I heard from Amma and Appa. They have never been happier in life. No apprehensions; only pure joy with Charlie, they had enough apprehensions with Abby and then Keethu, it appeared to me from what they were talking that Charlie was the daughter in law they have been waiting all these years.

When I saw Charlie at the airport, I almost fainted. Charlie's Indianisation was out of the world, she was wearing her usual Wrangler and casual white kurti, no all-American tees, and a small 'pottu' or 'bindi on her forehead and beautiful ear rings dangling from her ears. She looked tired but beautiful and stunning.

I could not control myself, shouted 'Charlie' and embraced her, she did the same thing and we hugged and kissed for eternity and broke away after realizing that we were the star attraction at the airport.

'Hey Jonnie...'

'Hey Charlie...'

We stood watching each for other for a long time.

'What are you watching?'

'You...you are more Indian than American...'

'Then what...I am Mrs. Charlie Janakiraman'

'You...you really pierced your ears...I can't believe it'

'Yeah, me too. One morning I woke up this crazy idea and told mom, she took me to GRT and here I am...' she dangled her ear rings. Typical Indian, Typical American Tamilian.

'Hey, what...you are looking at me like that...I have one more surprise for you'

'What is that?', I got close to her.

'Give me your ears...Hmm...you are going to be Papa soon'

First, it didn't register...

'What, did I hear you...'

'Yep honey. You heard me. I missed my period last month...'

'Ho, Ho...Did you go the Doctor?'

'No, not in India but tested with home kit. It came positive'

'Wonderful...ha...ha...oh my God...did you tell Amma, Appa?'

'No, I wanted you to the be first person to hear it'

'Oh, Charlie, I am over the moon. We are going to be parents finally. I will fix up the Doctor's appointment right away.

*

We waited expectantly till the Gynaecologist completed the all check-ups and tests. She finally addressed us with a pleasant smile.

'Mr. and Mrs. Shahas, I have good news for you. Mrs. Sahas is pregnant with twins, 7 weeks old and they both seem to be in good condition'

'Gee, twins...,' we both shouted excitedly.

'And their hearts have formed and are functioning smoothly. Here are the instructions for you to follow and meet me once every month for your regular check-up. Follow normal work life, eat well and sleep well'

Amma and Appa were ecstatic and even Athimber seemed to be happy. Whatever gifts one gets in life, there is nothing compared to God's gift. Baby. One's life becomes fulfilled only when they experience parenting. Noting else can be compared to this pleasure. One can be a son, or daughter or brother or sister, but being a father or mother beats everything else.

From then on I was traveling in a time machine. I wanted to hire a full-time maid as Charlie was thirty-four years old so that she can be taken care of well but she would not have any of it. She said she can take of herself and wanted to be physically active as long as she can. Her wish became my command.

'Honey, you have been waiting for this badly, right?'

'Yes, darling for long...'

I knew she was referring to what happened with Keethu and I held her hand tightly. We sat together with Charlie resting her head on my shoulder, contently for a long time drowned in our dreams blissfully. I was coming home as early as my work would permit and took Charlie for a walk in the evening around the neighbourhood every day and the next milestone was upon us even before we could even blink, her Baby Shower. We decided it is time to celebrate and I went the whole nine yards to make it happen and arranged for a grand function in JW Marriot, in typical Tamil Brahmin custom. The function hall was decorated like a mini temple. Amma, Appa, Akka and Athimber flew down from Chennai and the plan was Akka and Athimber would go back to India after the function, Amma and Appa would stay for six months and enjoy the time with the grandchildren. All friends and colleagues including Ravi, Chandran, Dave, Derrick, Gaby, Meghna etc., and about one hundred people graced the occasion.

Charlie was dressed in a designer lehenga and gagra choli because of her big tummy and dressing her in the madisar was a big challenge, so we dropped the idea. She looked half Indian and so beautiful with all the Manjal and Kumkum, flower in the head and garlands and the beautiful 'jimikkis' dangling to add grace every time she nodded or turned her head. Amma and Appa were so happy as if they got themselves a Tamil brahmin Mattuppen. Lunch was special Tamil Nadu sappadu served in plantain leaves and it was a marvellous sight watching all Americans relish the food with hand. Sweet Pongal, Jamun and appalam were the favourites.

*

The D day was upon us even before we realised. We admitted Charlie to the hospital as her labour pain started. The Doctor tried for a normal delivery as much as possible but due to her age, she could not and it was a C section that delivered the kids to us. I was waiting impatiently to see Charlie and the babies but had to wait for a couple of hours for Charlie to regain consciousness.

I went into the room with so much anxiety and anticipation. Charlie was barely conscious and smiled weakly at me. I was choking with anxiety and was close to tears.

'Charlie...'

'Honey...'

I bent and embraced her lightly and kissed on her lips. She pointed towards the cradle and I saw the twin bundle of joy and again was overwhelmed with emotion. I watched the babies for what it felt like an eternity.

The boy was elder and girl was younger as per the order of delivery and we named them Surya Chandra and Suhasini Chandra.

****

THIRTEEN

Chapter 13 – Home Coming!

'Honey, I wanted to ask you this for so long...'

'Shoot Dear...'

'Have you ever thought of moving back to India?'

'No, why are you asking?'

'I have been thinking how it would be when we start living in India'

'When did you start thinking about this?'

'As soon as Surya and Suhasini were born...'

'That's a long time...they are three years old now...why you didn't talk to me about it?'

'You have a great career here, I did not want that to be affected'

'Hmm... how serious are you about living in India?'

'I like India very much...'

'Aha, you have been to India only twice and seen hardly anything'

'But the memories keep flooding my mind of wherever I visited. India is vibrant and incredible'

'Visiting India for a vacation is very different from living there full time'

'Every place we went, it looked different but the feel was the same everywhere. The mood is always uplifting and people are very helpful'

'Yeah, the Sun shines there all through the year'

'I understand that makes India and Asia easy to live and Asians age slowly compared to the white people'

'That's correct brown skins ages slowly and wrinkles appear in the face way after people turn fifty'

'I also want to age slowly and I want the sun on my face every day, not like here in the US'

'So, that's your motivation, sun on your face every day...?'

'That plus the busy neighbourhood and the colourful festivals'

'Hmm...but it could be very crowded everywhere you go'

'I can manage it'

'It will dusty and no so hygienic like US'

'I will follow a rigorous hygiene practice'

'The traffic could be terrible'

'You are there to drive me around or we can hire a driver. You told me many a times that manpower is cheap in India'

'You have thought through all the angles. Have you not?'

'Yep, of course. It is a big decision. I know people would either be baffled or consider me insane'

'That's true. It has never happened. If we pull it off, we would be part of the elite group who did this before us'

'So American women have migrated to India?'

'Yeah, may be a handful'

'I don't mind joining the elite group'

'Hmm...Do you think the kids would adopt there?'

'They are only kids, they will adopt anywhere'

'What will we tell them when throw grow up'

'They are US citizens, they can come back to study here or work here or stay in India itself. Whatever they like'

'Well, that's possible'

'Jonnie, will you get a transfer to India? Or get a job in India?'

'Job in India, I don't know. As far as the transfer goes I can try, after all I was involved with India operations'

'Can you explore that?'

'Give me some time to think through this. I didn't expect this...It's kind of sudden'

'Sure thing, take your time'

'I need to tell you upfront even if I try for an India position it may not materialise immediately'

'Understood, when it comes through which city it will be'

'Obviously Bangalore'

'Wow, I love Bangalore'

*

I got busy with work and she with the babies and we did not discuss the subject for some time. The ever-perseverant Charlie brought it up in a couple of months' times.

'Jonnie, did you think through it?'

I was thinking of something else and I asked absent mindedly, 'About what?'

'About migrating to India'

'Oh, yeah. Let me ask you again. Are you serious?'

'I am dead serious'

'How about your parents, what will they say?'

'It's my life, they would not interfere but I am sure Amma and Appa would be exhilarated when they hear this'

'You have understood them very well but life in India would be chaotic'

'But did you not tell that Bangalore is the Silicon Valley of India?'

'Yes, it is'

'Are there Americans living and working in India?'

'Yep, not only Americans, a lot of Europeans too'

'If it works for them, it will work for me too'

'But they are there for a couple of years there or max three or four years, not lifelong'

'I don't mind living there for the rest of my life'

'Charlie, it is an irreversible process. Once we migrate, no going back. Think through and let me know in a week'

*

I spoke to my Manager who set the process in motion of finding me a role in India. Role for a Vice President cannot be found or created in a day, it takes months. The fact the I played a strong role in scaling up Bangalore operations was definitely an advantage.

Charlie was very happy that I agreed to migrate to India, actually it should have been the other way around. I should have been the one asking her about migrating to India.

Charlie started preparing Surya and Suhasini for living in India by showing photos of her India trip, Bangalore and Chennai and the bed time stories were all about India. They used to ask all kind of questions that only kids can ask, the most important being why it is very different there; whether they understood whatever they were hearing or seeing or not but they understood clearly that they are going to India.

In the meanwhile, Charlie became pregnant again.

'Charlie, do you want the third baby?'

'Of course, Jonnie. I would not think of otherwise. Why you don't want the third kid?'

'No, no... You are already fully tied up with taking care of Surya and Sini. I was wondering how will you manage the third one'

'It's God's gift, I will manage and you are there to take care of all of us'

'You are talking like a typical Indian woman'

'I am half Indian anyways'

That settled the matter.

My break came through when Charlie was six months pregnant. I got a good role managing a Business Unit from India Delivery Centre.

I needed to move to India in a month's time and take over the role.

'Jonnie, when will you take us?'

'Let me join there and find a house and apply for visa etc., etc.,'

'How long will that take?'

'Maybe a couple of months if not three'

'Then I can be in India for the delivery'

'Hmm...I don't think it is a good idea'

'Why?'

'If the baby is born in India, he or she will be an Indian citizen'

'So what, you are Indian'

'I guess it would be better for all the kids to be American citizens. I don't want the third kid to feel different when he or she grows up'

'Do you think it really makes a difference?'

'This is matter of our kid's life. I don't want to make a mistake and regret later'

'Hmm…what do you suggest?'

'You deliver the baby in here Unites States. Then all five of us go to India together and settle down there'

'Okies, whatever you say honey because you are a wise man'

*

I flew to India a month later as per plan and took over my new role. It took me a month to navigate the India corporate workplace. I had to unlearn a lot especially not to think like an American and really understand the Indian thinking. I was wondering, 'Am I not Indian? Why I am struggling like my fellow Americans?'. This is what living in United States does to anyone, everybody else feel Alien. I found Bangalore was not only a cosmopolitan city but a global one, the vibes were the same as across major cities in the world. It was not only the IT Capital of India but the Pub capital too and I heard that new trend was the microbreweries. I was taken to one such new swanky microbrewery and found it interesting. All my team members were working hard and smart and the one thing I found lacking was the accountability. I guess that was ingrained in Indian culture and it is going to be a big challenge for me to work on.

In the meanwhile, I rented a big 5 bed room villa in Whitefield for a fraction of a rent it would cost me in the United States and started furnishing it as per Charlie's instructions. I got a company leased Toyota Innova and a good driver to drive me around. I was still not ready to drive myself on Indian roads again. But I knew I have to bite the bullet sooner or later.

Before I could blink, Charlies' delivery was due. I flew into Philly just in time to welcome our third baby and it was a beautiful girl. We felt the same exhilaration in receiving the new baby as we received the twins. We named her Surabhi and every moment we spent with her was pure bliss, Surya and Sini were always fighting to be near Surabhi. So, Charlie worked out a rota that let each of them assist Charlie to take care of Surabhi.

I felt a sudden feeling of fulfilment and felt grateful, I can not say why or explain the feeling but it was definitely because of Surabhi. Having three-year-old twins was enjoyment at the best, but Surabhi's arrival made me feel more responsible, making me a vow to take care of her very well. All of them. Last born children are always special because they are the youngest but I felt that alone was not the case with Surabhi, something more of divine love.

We checked with the Paediatrician as to how soon Surabhi can travel to India and she advised us to take her after she completes one month. I decided to work from Unites States for that period and took care of winding up in the United States. We sold both the cars and all furniture and appliances, rented out Charlie's flat, taking only clothes, medicine for Surabhi and the kids and other essentials.

Charlie got excited as the travel date was approaching and the enthusiasm infected all of us and finally the D day was upon us. We travelled to the airport in sheer anticipation and excitement and checked in and cleared security. It felt that every action was taking us closer to India. When the boarding was announced, we were the first to board and business class cabin crew took extra care to settle us especially Charlie and Surabhi. I settled alongside with Surya and Sini. In flight services started in a while and I was content to sip single malt and enjoy my meal. I helped Charlie to eat and Surya and Sini were managing themselves well despite that being their first flight journey. They were all the more excited to watch the lights or dark sky outside.

It was time to sleep, before the cabin crew switched off the lights Charlie smiles at me knowingly as to what was going in my mind. She knows me too well. My mind started racing backwards, fifteen years back and the flashback started playing in my mind. The day I landed unconscious on the aircraft ladder, my induction in the American bar, first day in office, first sex, first date and first love. Then I thought of Abby and the painful divorce and MIT, my big job after the M.S., and Keethu. I could confidently say that I have seen it all and done it all. I have a Green Card and American Passport but that does not make me less Indian. I am going home. It felt strange to say I am going home. I had embraced United States as my home and thought so until that moment in the flight, on the way to India.

My company had given me a two-year assignment, either renewable or I go back to Unites States if I wanted to. Made it flexible.

But I am not going back; with that clarity a sudden calmness engulfed me and I closed my eyes and went to sleep.

****

Previous Works by Mohan K Thangaraju
One Midnight Summer Madness

Every sin begins with a secret. Every redemption begins with truth.

When Bhaskaran aka "Bazz" — a brilliant and ambitious corporate strategist — crosses a forbidden line one midnight, sexually penetrates his lovable niece, Shalini, only seventeen, his life unravels in ways he never imagined. The man who once ruled boardrooms and headlines soon finds himself behind bars, condemned not just by law, but by his own conscience and family.

From the gleaming towers of Bangalore's Corporate world to the stark silence of a prison cell, *One Midnight Summer Madness* is a haunting confession of guilt, obsession, and redemption. Told through the fragmented memories of a man seeking forgiveness in captivity, the novel explores how a single act of weakness can destroy a lifetime of achievement — and yet, how even in darkness, the search for meaning endures.

Blending emotional intensity with moral complexity, Mohan K Thangaraju delivers a deeply human story of ambition, love, and repentance. With its unflinching honesty and cinematic depth, *One Midnight Summer Madness* stands as one of his most powerful works — a reminder that the past never forgets, and the heart never fully heals.

Fool's Paradise

Love can be truth. It can also be illusion.

Ram K Prakash has lived a full life — successful, admired, and adored. Yet behind the façade of achievement lies a lifetime of deception, desire, and disquiet. Torn between the wife, Shanthi, who grounds him; the lover, Chandra, who consumes him, and the woman who understands his soul, Ram moves through the decades convinced he can control his heart — until the illusions collapse, leaving him to face the truth of who he has become.

Set against the rapidly changing landscape of modern India, *Fool's Paradise* explores the quiet tragedy of a man who mistakes longing for love and illusion for happiness. In his most confessional work, Mohan K. Thangaraju dissects the fragility of human relationships with piercing insight and emotional honesty. A moving portrait of love, loss, and self-deception, *Fool's Paradise* reminds us that the hardest truths are the ones we tell ourselves.

www.ingramcontent.com/pod-product-compliance
Lightning Source LLC
Chambersburg PA
CBHW062217150726
47991CB00006B/2322